FLOWERS
OF GRASS

Embracing Family
Nobuo Kojima

Realm of the Dead
Uchida Hyakken

The Budding Tree: Six Stories of Love in Edo
Aiko Kitahara

The Temple of the Wild Geese and Bamboo Dolls of Echizen
Tsutomu Mizukami

The Glass Slipper and Other Stories
Shotaro Yasuoka

The Word Book
Mieko Kanai

Isle of Dreams
Keizo Hino

Plainsong
Kazushi Hosaka

The Shadow of a Blue Cat
Naoyuki Ii

Building Waves
Taeko Tomioka

TAKEHIKO FUKUNAGA

FLOWERS
OF GRASS

TRANSLATED AND WITH AN AFTERWORD
BY ROYALL TYLER

DALKEY ARCHIVE PRESS
CHAMPAIGN • DUBLIN • LONDON

Originally published in Japanese as *Kusa no hana* by Shinchosha, Tokyo, 1954

Library of Congress Cataloging-in-Publication Data

Fukunaga, Takehiko, 1918-1979.
[Kusa no hana. English]
Flowers of grass / Takehiko Fukunaga ; translated by Royall Tyler. -- 1st ed.
   p. cm.
ISBN 978-1-56478-714-9 (pbk. : alk. paper)
I. Tyler, Royall. II. Title.
PL850.K8K813 2012
895.6'35--dc23
                              2012001868

Partially funded by a grant from the Illinois Arts Council, a state agency

This book has been selected by the Japanese Literature Publishing Project (JLPP), an initiative
of the Agency for Cultural Affairs of Japan

www.dalkeyarchive.com

Cover: design and composition by Sarah French
Printed on permanent/durable acid-free paper and bound in the United States of America

*For all flesh is as grass, and all the glory of man
as the flower of grass.*

1 PETER 1:24

Winter

That crape myrtle tree fascinated me. It stood all by itself in the garden area behind the auditorium, Jukō Hall. Once a month or so the sanatorium patients were treated to a movie in Jukō Hall, although I myself, not yet being fully recovered, never actually went to see one there. I strolled around the grounds only on days of warm winter sun, without too much wind. Kerria roses, camellias, and maples grew there around a pond. Two or three ilex trees by the windows at the back of Jukō Hall were as green and round as the trees in a Douanier Rousseau painting. Across from them stood a row of lifeless plum trees, and in the middle, next to an arbor, that solitary crape myrtle.

The crape myrtle bared its branches eerily to the sky—naked branches, dead-looking, smooth. I couldn't resist running my hand over them when I approached it, almost spellbound: smooth as a baby's skin they were, but at the same time unpleasantly old. Unbelievably, in summer they put out countless tiny leaves and, for a hundred days, clusters of red flowers. Now, though, they reached meaninglessly for the heavens like a hundred twisted hands. This tree was completely unrelated to anything else in the world.

I had already spent two winters here at this sanatorium in Kiyose, on the outskirts of Tokyo. The first winter I underwent thoracoplastic surgery, from which I recuperated so slowly that I couldn't take a walk outside until the following autumn. For that reason I'd never seen the garden behind the Jukō Hall in summer—never seen the crape myrtle tree covered in summer leaves and flowers. For all I knew, it always spread its twisty branches there naked and alone. (This was five years ago. Later on I saw it in full summer bloom, but by that time it no longer mattered to me.)

Once I visited the tree with Shiomi Shigeshi. I kept my hands in the folds of my padded kimono for warmth, while Shiomi, wearing a coat over his white hospital gown, had his hands deep in its pockets. As usual I stroked one of the branches. Colder than the surrounding air, it twisted about like life itself.

"Nature's scary, isn't it," I said. "Look at the way it stays alive."

"It's a crape myrtle?" he asked.

"That's right. You didn't know? Come spring it'll be covered with buds, and in the summer it'll flower. The whole thing's a mystery to me."

Shiomi was about to have an operation, so I suppose I may have meant my commonplace remark to boost his morale. I myself hardly knew whether summer would ever actually come or not. Everyone wants to get better, of course, but a sick man who's already suffered a lot never forgets that recovery is beyond his control. There might never be a summer.

"It's ridiculous," Shiomi retorted. "What's the point of being alive and miserable like this? I'll take being dead any time. This thing is faking death already."

He lifted his foot and kicked the trunk with the teeth of his wooden geta. That seemed to take it all out of him. "Let's go," he said.

The back gate next to the mortuary fascinated me, too. A footpath circled the hospital complex. The lush summer grass was dead at this time of year, and the oaks and chestnuts that bordered it had dropped their leaves. From the path you could see the hospital rooms, and bedridden patients in them could make out, beyond the leafless trees, a scattering of shingle-roof fresh-air pavilions.

The mortuary stood well apart among the trees, at a spot on the path from which you could no longer see the hospital building at all. Past the entrance door, which was always locked, you stepped into a space with an earthen floor. An eight-mat room beyond it contained an altar, and next to it was a six-mat waiting room. At the back, on the other side of a thick wall, was the autopsy room. The building awaited new arrivals with the malevolence of fate.

One winter morning we were leaning on the windowsill of our room, looking out. Two nurses and the old fellow in charge of the mortuary were carrying a body on a stretcher. A bank of gray, freezing clouds hung low, and a sun like a blot of ink shed a feeble light while frost gathered on the white blanket over the corpse. One or two relatives followed in silence as the procession headed slowly toward the mortuary.

We leaned on the windowsill and watched. The voices of the nurses carrying the stretcher reached us through the biting air. We couldn't make out what they were saying, but they certainly were talking—sometimes even laughing. What could they be laughing about? They seemed not to have a care in the world.

"What a nerve!" I exclaimed.

"They're just doing their job," Kaku said. "For them it's *routine*." He used the English word. Kaku was a mechanic. Completely self-taught, he read technical works in English and sometimes slipped English into his conversation.

"There's a time and place for everything, though. What on earth do they think they're carrying?"

"Tanaka's the one in front," Kaku went on. Nurse Tanaka, we all agreed, was a beauty. She never cracked a smile in a patient's presence, but she often laughed with the girls. You sometimes heard her laugh when you passed the nurses' lounge room.

"The prig!" I muttered. "I can't stand a silly girl."

The voices and the procession receded into the distance. "She's not silly," Shiomi remarked to no one in particular, "she's just young."

I turned around. He was sitting cross-legged on his bed, smoking a cigarette.

"Those nurses are alive, that's all," he said. "Other people dying or not doesn't concern them. A corpse is a corpse. They're alive. They laugh, they cry—that's all. Their world has nothing to do with dead people. 'Like moths fluttering around the lamp of death,' a poet like you might say."

I hardly knew what to say. Meanwhile, the procession had moved out of sight. That night, during the wake before the coffin laid out in the mortuary, I saw Tanaka the prig wipe tears from her eyes.

A lot of patients died that winter. This was five years ago. Streptomycin was just becoming available then, but it was expensive, and not everyone could afford it. Orthopedic surgery was common enough, but pneumonectomy lagged well behind. It was a hard winter, and many died. I saw body after body go by.

Nonetheless, the back gate would always be securely shut when I took the path to the mortuary lurking there in the woods. Every time I pushed absentmindedly with both hands against its square, rough timbers. It creaked a little then, but it never opened. The barked, jagged verticals and crosspieces sturdily barred my way. No, that gate opened only to admit and release the hearse—in other words, only on those occasions when we lined up before the mortuary to see the coffin off, as we put it. For the sanatorium's seven hundred patients there were only two ways out: through the front gate, or through the back. Most left through the front gate, but some went out the back. I could never repress a surge of dark rage when I gave that gate a shove. I never went to it with Shiomi Shigeshi, but I just knew that if he'd been with me he'd have pushed at it—that gate of doom, so to speak—with a fury far greater than mine. Just as the crape myrtle and the back gate by the mortuary fascinated me, a single idea possessed him. What distinguished him from the rest of us at the sanatorium was that this idea concerned not his own death, but that of others. Unfortunately, I understood that only much too late.

I didn't start writing this just to talk about myself, though. I only mean to introduce the man named Shiomi Shigeshi.

For not quite a year I occupied the sanatorium bed next to his. It was a "big room," as they called it: six beds. Patients on the mend would go out to the fresh-air pavilions for exercise or work therapy; those on the way down would go off to individual rooms. So there was some turnover in a big room. During my stay in the sanatorium I shared the room with a dozen people. I can say that for a while I enjoyed with each of them a friendship due entirely to chance. In the daytime we six shared our daily anxieties, and at night our fears. Naturally we were close friends. "For a while," I said—but, really, what friendship is not just "for a while"? Nonetheless, each of us had his own solitude: a solitude over which he bent, as though weighing it, on his side of a blank wall. Besides, we all differed in age, past experience, and physical condition, and none of us could claim that no feelings of jealousy, envy, malice, or, especially, egotism lurked in the cracks between us.

The misfortune that afflicted the sanatorium patients had generally come on them as a complete shock, one that had changed the course of their lives. Just when they could pride themselves on their good health, the disease had swept down on them like a gust of wind and blown off their hats. Now they were chasing those rolling hats, and in their frantic effort to catch up with them, they had gradually lost sight of what it was really like to be alive. Nowhere else is "to be alive" whispered with such deep feeling, but in practice, anxiety about their condition had shrunk its meaning for them to matters of sputum examination, X-ray photography, surgical diagnosis, or measurement of blood sedimentation. Just as each had his own medical chart, so each bore the scars and the special solitude inflicted on him by his own condition. No assurances of improvement from the doctor could allay a patient's misgivings. Medically speaking, there is almost never any certainty that a patient has recovered completely. The highest degree of comfort—that so-and-so is doing better or worse than somebody else—is still only relative. And even after physical recovery, the associated psychological injury is likely to last the rest of the patient's life. Awareness of this injury further intensified our loneliness.

Shiomi Shigeshi appealed to me above all because his strength of spirit never allowed this injury to show. Although I slept in the bed next to his, I never once saw him upset about a turn for the worse. The blood sedimentation test and sputum examination were done once a month. The blood was taken before breakfast, and the results came in between nine and ten o'clock. Someone from our room would then sneak into the nurses' office, out of sight of the doctors, and copy out the score for each of us six. Only the college student we called Ryō-chan always got a good rating; for the rest of us it went up and down. The results of the sputum examination took a few days during which we waited on pins and needles, murmuring among ourselves that we were certainly done for this time. They were graded from one to ten on the Gaffky scale, and an absence of bacteria was registered as a minus. Ryō-chan usually got a minus, while Shiomi or Kaku, the mechanic, often came out with a five or six. I'd jump for joy at a minus, but at a mere plus one I'd lie down and hide under the covers. Shiomi, though, would just grunt in acknowledgement, however bad his result, and his expression betrayed nothing at all.

"How can you take it so calmly?" I asked.

"Just as long as my spirit's alive . . ." he answered. "What I'm like is my business."

"Fine! But this spirit of yours—doesn't your physical deterioration ever weaken it?"

"The body decays, I know that. And that's precisely why I prefer to look after my spirit. You, too, I expect."

"But how can you bear to watch your physical being slowly fail? There's no spirit left to look after, you know, once the body's dead."

"Watching that way means being alive," he said, unfazed.

"You're splitting hairs." That was the best I could come up with.

"You're all sensibility. That's what a poet's like, I suppose. Me, I just live by observing."

Actually, I *had* been writing poems since I was a boy, but all the same I had no wish to be treated as a poet, so I made a face and said no more. Shiomi took out a pack of cigarettes he kept hidden under his pillow and lit one. He coughed, then inhaled deeply again.

"I used to be like you," he said, "but then I killed off my sensibility. No, not my sensibility, exactly—more my soul. I envy you."

For a while a dark look settled over his face.

Shiomi first joined our room when I was recuperating badly from thoracoplasty and spending all my time lying on my back in a corner bed. Spring was coming on at last, and the song of a lark was pouring down from high in the blue sky framed by the window. No other sound broke the silence of the hospital's afternoon rest period. I was daydreaming, my head turned toward the window, when a hospital trolley came rattling down the corridor toward the room, the door opened, and two nurses brought in a set of bedding. The patient in the bed next to mine had moved a few days before to a fresh-air pavilion, and the mattress was bare. I wondered what the new neighbor would be like, but the nurses' bustling about was more annoying than I was curious. I pulled the covers over my head and dropped off to sleep.

A nurse woke me up. Ah, I said to myself, time for my temperature. With a yawn I reported a temperature of 36.8°C and a pulse of 78. Then I happened to glance toward the next bed. Empty till a moment ago, it was now spread with a new quilt. A man in a white gown sat cross-legged on it, calmly smoking a cigarette.

"Your temperature?" the nurse inquired.

"How about next time? I haven't taken it yet."

The nurse (a conscientious young trainee) stared at the fellow in some confusion, then moved on irresolutely to the next bed. She noted the temperature of the three patients opposite and was already on her way out of the room when she turned back with a determined look and said, "Mr. Shiomi, don't you know you're not allowed to smoke?"

"I'm aware of that," he answered without missing a beat.

The nurse stared at him, chuckled, and rushed out.

I laughed.

"You're pretty cocky," I remarked.

"I'm Shiomi. Pleased to meet you," he said formally. "As far as I can see, you just made your temperature up, so I assumed she wouldn't worry about my smoking." He let out a satisfied puff. "I've just moved in, after all. Surely they can allow me just one."

Smoking was naturally prohibited throughout the sanatorium, but patients on the mend were sorely tempted. Kaku, in the middle bed opposite, had a collapsed lung that gave ample cause for concern, but as he sat on his bed amid rows of radio parts, wielding his soldering iron, he smoked on the sly. Then there was the window bed on my side, where a fiftyish fellow we called Pop proudly refused to give up the habit of a lifetime. He was some sort of junk dealer, and he'd seen everything, good or bad. His wife came to visit him, hand in hand with their small child, on days when the business was closed. During the rest period all three of them would go for a walk, and he'd sometimes come back smelling slightly of drink.

Smoking was Shiomi Shigeshi's only bad habit. He'd steal a smoke with obvious pleasure whenever the nurses and doctors weren't around.

"Shiomi, won't you please stop smoking? It really bothers me when I'm resting." This was Ryō-chan.

"It bothers you? Does the smoke really get all the way over there?"

"It bothers me, that's all. Besides, it's crazy, smoking in a sanatorium."

Ryō-chan sat up on his bed. His round face, normally the picture of health, was deathly pale. Generally he just lay there right in front of me, corpselike, without a word, but at times he'd become insanely jolly, humming tunes and teasing the nurses. His excitement would then die down, like a wind, and he'd lapse back

16

into gloomy silence. This happened repeatedly. He was an odd young man. He'd been a medical student, but he was so frantically nervous about his own condition that despite always being the leading candidate for release into the fresh air, he renounced the privilege by complaining, every time a doctor examined him, about how ill he felt. His experience in medical school might certainly have taught him caution, but he suffered from the fixed conviction that his condition really was very serious and that the doctors just failed to understand it.

"It's crazy, I know," Shiomi replied, "but I'd prefer it if you'd let me take care of myself."

"Anyone who does things bad for his health and doesn't care is crazy," Ryō-chan insisted.

"I don't see the problem, as long as it doesn't do anyone else any harm. Does it *really* bother you, or do you just think smoking itself is crazy?"

"Both, you moron." He was shaking.

Shiomi calmly went on smoking with obvious enjoyment. "Are you that desperate not to die?" he asked quietly, peering at Ryō-chan's face. An awkward silence filled the room.

"All right, all right," I interrupted, "bickering *is* bad for you."

Ryō-chan lay down again with the covers over his head. Kaku, bent over a radio, went on extracting chirping sounds from it as though nothing had happened. I see, I said to myself: the real object of Ryō-chan's anger had been Kaku. Their beds were side by side, and there was constant trouble between them. Kaku had an angular face like a shogi piece, and his hair was already thinning, but he and Ryō-chan were much the same age. His medical condition was bad, and it showed, but even so he was always up, working away at his job, repairing radios. He had been through a lot since childhood, he was stubborn, and he could take it. Basically, he was a frank, simple man. The smoke reaching Ryō-chan actually came from Kaku's old pipe.

Well then, I thought, he should have been angry with Kaku. Still, he must have had *some* reason for barking at Shiomi instead. Shiomi's unflappable manner and his calm acceptance of his condition, however serious, as though it didn't personally concern him, must have struck Ryō-chan every time as a covert rebuke. To us, Shiomi's indifference toward his own life felt in a way completely unreal. He could have slipped into our sanatorium room without being ill at all. Presumably that was why he inspired friendship in me, awe in Kaku and Pop, and jealousy in Ryō-chan. All of us feared death and the shadow of death; only Shiomi seemed detached and free. In reality, though, he was deeply in thrall to the same fear. He just didn't let himself show it.

My friendly feeling toward Shiomi was probably due in part to our having both studied at the same university at about the same time. We hadn't known each other then, because I was majoring in foreign literatures and he in linguistics. Still, the knowledge that we'd very likely passed each other on the same gingko-lined avenue, or stood side by side before the shelves of the same secondhand bookstores, did much to bring us together. I seriously doubt, though, that he returned the friendship I was coming to feel for him. Sometimes he joked and made people laugh. He was a good talker when he felt like it. However, a kind of solitude always seemed to envelop him. He never really opened up to me, even in intimate conversation. Moreover, he never said a word about his past, so that I had no idea what the source of his loneliness might be.

That winter was the hardest that I spent in the sanatorium. When I woke up in the middle of the night, the freezing wind howling through the darkness conveyed utter desolation. Freezing air entered through the still-open window. Far away, in another room, someone was coughing his life away. Through those long, sleepless nights, the bottle of mouthwash on my night table gradually froze.

The monotonous days rolled by. On the coldest of them, under a leaden sky, we kept entirely to our beds except for meals. A hand protruding from under the covers grew numb with cold, and the book on the reading stand remained stuck forever at the same page. You lacked the will to do or think anything at all. Endless trains of associated images, all of them unbearably depressing, led off into past memory or future fantasy. No boy's dreams of the life ahead could have envisaged our miserable present. The very expression "to be alive" inevitably implies a burning openness to joy and sorrow. For us, though, living consisted only of getting through one day, then another, with nothing to do and nothing to think, in a state of dreary lassitude. The sadness of having strayed from the proper path of life brought with it many practical difficulties and weighed heavily on all of us.

"You're certainly getting a lot of work done," I remarked.

Shiomi had set up a desk on his bed and was filling a notebook with writing. Actually, it was less a desk than a roughly adapted tangerine crate. He rested an elbow on it, turned toward me, and laughed.

"This isn't work," he said.

"*I* can't get it together to do a damn thing, though. People keep telling me I'm lucky, you can write poetry in bed. No way! What kind of mindless stuff could you possibly write in bed?"

"You *do* have things to write about, though, don't you?"

"Things to write about isn't the problem. Once you have them, you have poetry. I'm just not up to getting them. It takes all you've got to write a single line of poetry, and I don't have that kind of energy. I envy you. What are you writing, though?"

"What am I writing?" He stopped short, looking slightly embarrassed. "Something like a novel, I suppose."

"Amazing! It's quite a struggle, isn't it."

He apparently thought I was being sarcastic. "Don't get me wrong, it's nothing fancy. You're a real poet, and you take poetry seriously enough to give it your best shot. In other words, you expect in time to do just that. For now you're storing up the honey of experience, so as to create things in the future. You're a dedicated specialist, you see—in short, an artist. Not me, though. I'm not writing to be published or read. It's just that I don't feel right unless I'm writing something to prove I'm still alive."

"So you're writing for yourself and no one else. That's great. I mean it."

"You're embarrassing me," he said.

Most of the time, the six of us were as quiet as mice. I struggled without much success through a book, turning a page now and again as though suddenly remembering what I was supposed to be doing. In the bed across from me Ryō-chan lay stock-still with a neatly folded towel over his eyes. Next to him Kaku worked discreetly at repairing broken radios. In the bed next to Kaku, by the window, a quiet youth whose slight stutter had put him in the habit of smiling when he listened to people, lay on his belly cutting mimeo stencils. The faint scratching of his steel stylus only deepened the silence. In the window bed on my side, Pop read a cheap magazine or dozed. Finally, between Pop and me, Shiomi sat at his desk, writing "something like a novel," and pausing now and again to enjoy a cigarette.

The room was not always deathly quiet, though. We were all bored, and a remark from any one of us might make the others sit up in their beds and start us talking interminably. Sometimes the talk turned into a discussion, or even an argument. The one most apt to speak sharply was Ryō-chan.

"Just stop it, will you?" Only his lips moved.

Kaku, in the bed next to him, was adjusting a radio. With a pained expression on his face he stopped. The radio began squealing.

"Take it easy, Ryō-chan," I said. I was always first in with an officious comment.

Ryō-chan took the towel off his eyes and glared at me.

"You're disturbing my rest!" he shouted.

Kaku turned the radio off and signaled me not to get him riled up. It drove me crazy, his being such a nice guy. He was always so damned considerate. Fixing radios and cutting stencils were about the only jobs the sanatorium allowed.

"You have no right to complain to Kaku," I said. "Just consider the social contradictions that force him to keep at his job."

"A sick man has no business working," he retorted. "Anyway, he's bothering me. Stop it!"

I need hardly say that we were all poor. Very few of the patients could afford their hospital stay on their own. Most were there thanks to remittances under the Livelihood Protection Law. Their admission fee was waived, and they received five hundred yen a month for expenses. For patients like Shiomi and me, there was medical assistance that covered just the admission fee. With a proper job you could get the health insurance that came with it, but that was good for only two years after the onset of the illness, so some patients had to leave the sanatorium before they had fully recovered. The young fellow with the stencils came under the Livelihood Protection scheme, but five hundred yen a month wasn't nearly enough to get by on. Kaku had paid a portion of the admission fee from his own pocket. The provisions of the Livelihood Protection Law were strict, the associated procedures were cumbersome, and a welfare officer's whim could easily block an application. In Kaku's case, the size of his parents' business alone decided the matter against him. He had defaulted on his admission fee, and he worked to earn his spending money. (I knew all about these things. You no longer have secrets from someone with whom you've shared for years a hospital room and even the aluminum utensils for the dismal hospital meals. I also knew that Kaku's parents' business was in dire straits and that Pop's little girl had a bad case of measles. I knew about Ryō-chan's love life. About Shiomi, though, I knew nothing at all.)

Once Ryō-chan lost his temper, there was no end to it. Kaku had put his radio equipment away, so he dug into me next.

"I'd appreciate it if other people would mind their own business," he announced. "I can do without advice from *you*, _____." (He used my family name).

"You *are* a bit selfish, you know," I answered with conscious restraint.

"Selfish? What are you talking about? Don't try playing big brother with me!"

His plump face looked rather comical.

"Ryō-chan," I told him, "you're always talking about getting enough rest, but how about giving a thought to your spiritual hygiene? Lack of spiritual balance endangers your body, too."

"I'm fine as I am. There you go again, meddling, right? What a busybody!"

"I wonder," I muttered and left it at that.

Shiomi put in a leisurely word of his own. "I'd say Ryō-chan's quite right to have a temper."

This caught me by surprise. Ryō-chan, who no doubt agreed secretly that he was indeed selfish, glanced at Shiomi in blank amazement.

"If you feel like yelling, you might as well go ahead—that's what I'd call spiritual hygiene." He turned to me and grinned. "If you feel like crying, cry. Laugh, if you feel like laughing. That's what's natural. But for some reason we've all been wrongly brought up to believe that virtue lies in repressing our feelings. I'm not claiming it's all right to be unreasonable, but after thinking it over a bit I realize how much harm it's done me not to cry when I wanted to cry, not to get angry when I felt like it. To be alive means to express yourself, to burn yourself up. To live fully, you have to set your emotions aflame. So Ryō-chan, as far as I can see, is living for all he's worth, and I really envy him. Of course"—here he dropped his voice—"that certainly *can* be a problem for other people."

Ryō-chan was lying down again with the bedclothes over his head. You couldn't tell whether Shiomi's sarcasm had affected him or not. After that, though, his outbursts became rather less frequent than before.

Our most animated discussions undoubtedly concerned our own medical condition, and among us all, it was Shiomi's state, and his coming operation, that attracted the greatest interest. The following diagnosis was written on his chart: "1 egg-sized cavity, upper right lobe hilum; dispersed seepage, mid-lower lobe; intermediate seepage, middle right lobe."

Shiomi had moved to our sanatorium after some time at a Christian church-affiliated one nearby. There were so many institutions of the kind, large and small—a dozen or so—in the immediate area that people called the place a hospital town. Shiomi's, one of the smaller ones, had lacked a surgical facility. A good many patients moved from there to ours for their operations.

At Shiomi's initial examination, the young doctor in charge examined the X-rays and Shiomi's face with equal care.

"I just can't tell whether the operation will succeed completely or not," he said. "The cavity's a real problem, you see."

"I want a pneumonectomy," Shiomi replied.

"A pneumonectomy? That might be all right if the other side was clear . . . It's a bit dangerous, isn't it?"

"But I want it."

Shiomi expressed himself so forcefully that the young doctor looked a little hurt. After the examination we talked the matter over in our usual way.

"You're incredibly brave, Shiomi." Kaku's admiring remark started things off. He said that even the weekly chest exam we all got made him nervous, and he shuddered even to think of surgery.

"I have the impression that pneumonectomy is still pretty risky," I said. "You'd better wait a while and see how things go."

"I mean to have the operation," Shiomi insisted.

"Surely thoracoplasty would do it," Pop put in.

"Thoracoplasty doesn't work." This time it was Ryō-chan. "Thoracoplasty could never get rid of a cavity like that."

"So what about pneumonectomy?" I inquired. Say what you like about Ryō-chan, he was still a medical student, and we respected his informed opinion.

"Absolutely not! It's too dangerous," Ryō-chan replied loudly. "Prolonged rest first and then a course of streptomycin might help to stabilize the site, but even then you can't be sure how it would go."

"It's what I'm going to have done, though," Shiomi declared, smiling but unyielding.

Admittedly, some seriously ill patients still managed to look healthy from the outside. Shiomi was a perfect example. He never ran the slightest fever, he coughed very little, and he was fully mobile. The sensible course for him was to skip the risky operation and lie around quietly, waiting to see how things worked out.

Our sanatorium topped the list of the local establishments that did offer lung surgery. Every member of the surgical staff was exceptionally keen on research and had a good deal of experience.

Dr. Murata, by far the youngest of those who wielded the scalpel there, was extremely popular with both patients and nurses. Unlike the others, he was never unapproachable. There was always an affable smile on his face. He knew so much about music that he took on introducing the pieces played for our record concerts, and with tweezers and medicine wrapping paper he would make the nurses origami cranes smaller than beans. However, it was the way he handled the scalpel on the operating table that really showed off his dexterity. His rapid, virtually error-free work inspired the patients' trust. They firmly believed that if Dr. Murata's surgery failed, the case had been hopeless anyway.

"All right, how'd it go?" we all asked Shiomi.

"Still undecided," he answered, looking a bit tired. "It seems success isn't impossible. As cases go it's an interesting one, he says."

"Dr. Murata doesn't seem to feel too sure of himself," Kaku remarked.

"He'd never perform that dangerous an operation," said Ryō-chan.

This type of surgery—pneumonectomy, the removal of an entire lobe of the lungs—was then only just entering medical practice. It was performed on patients beyond the help of thoracoplasty, but there were few suitable candidates for it, and also few who wanted it. A thoracoplasty operation could be done in under an hour, but a pneumonectomy took ten and so required unusual resolve on the part of both the surgeon and the patient. Streptomycin could not be used freely because it was rationed, and blood transfusions depended on the availability of qualified nurses. Nowadays hardly anyone dies from either operation. Back then, though, to submit yourself to a pneumonectomy you had to be ready for death. A patient approached on the subject usually objected strenuously before finally agreeing. It was very rare for someone to insist on the operation himself, as Shiomi was doing. If I'd been Ryō-chan, I'd have retorted sarcastically, "Are you really *that* desperate to get better?" However, Shiomi had a strange toughness that put him beyond the reach of any sarcasm.

The winter continued. In late December the first snow fell, and even colder weather then took us into the New Year. There was nothing in all of sanatorium life as miserably lonely as New Year's. Each patient got a festive rice cake and a box of simple New Year's delicacies, and on the last day of the year a little charcoal was passed out to each room. On New Year's morning the kitchen sent us a pot of broth, which we made into *zōni* soup over a small charcoal stove. Pop had leave to go home for the occasion, and the five of us who stayed behind celebrated the day very modestly. It felt very much like all the other days of the year. The only difference was that after nightfall Kaku mentioned playing cards with the nurses on duty and went off to the nurses' station to put the idea to them. Then one day followed another again in monotonous succession.

It was after January seventh, I think, that I went one day for a stroll outside and spent some time chatting with a young poet friend in one of the fresh-air pavilions. He suddenly asked, as though the thought had only just popped into his head, "There's this fellow named Shiomi—he isn't by chance one of your roommates, is he?"

"Yes, he is. His bed is next to mine."

"There's a odd story about him. Perhaps I shouldn't repeat it."

I remembered that my companion had moved to our sanatorium from the same smaller one as Shiomi. Curiosity got the better of me, and I urged him to go on.

"He attempted suicide, you see, and there was a big fuss about it. It was about this time the year before last. He suddenly disappeared from the ward. Foreign missionaries run the place, and they're very strict about anyone leaving or spending the night elsewhere. Anyway, Shiomi's condition was serious, and he'd been completely bedridden. He couldn't possibly just get up and leave. Something was obviously wrong. He disappeared around midday, wearing only a jacket and an overcoat over his hospital gown, and by dinnertime he still wasn't back. Everyone went out looking for him."

"You, too?"

"No, I wasn't well enough yet. I stayed in bed."

"So what happened? Did they find him?"

"You know what? He just came strolling in all by himself, after lights out. He said he hadn't been up to it after all, and he'd just been wandering around in the woods behind Mount Sankaku."

"Did he have poison with him or something?"

"I don't know. He never had much to say, anyway. Has he changed at all?"

"I wouldn't call him especially untalkative. He's pretty normal. This just doesn't make any sense."

"The sanatorium director got really worried about him. I imagine that night was why Shiomi ended up being baptized."

"You mean he's a Christian? I had no idea. He has absolutely nothing to do with the YMCA types around here."

"Really? I suppose the director was so afraid of having a suicide on his hands, he just about forced Shiomi to accept baptism. You can't kill yourself, you see, once you're a Christian."

"Mm. He's strange, though, Shiomi. This doesn't sound like him at all."

Back in the room again, I couldn't bring myself to mention the matter to Shiomi. During the winter he went two or three times to Dr. Murata's office. Through the nurses we heard that the issue of his operation had aroused intense debate at a meeting of the medical staff. In the end, the decision went Shiomi's way. The operation was scheduled for mid-February.

"Wouldn't you *like* to try your hand at a case like mine?" Shiomi said he'd asked Dr. Murata.

"Of course I would. I'd like to have a go at a lot of such cases. There are just so few people who want the operation." Dr. Murata smiled.

"Then go ahead. I'll be quite satisfied if my body serves to further medical progress."

"All right, but you see, if there *should* be any danger to you, as a doctor I . . ."

"I'm the patient, though, and I'm telling you that it doesn't matter. You have nothing at all to worry about. I'll sign a waiver, if you like."

Shiomi told us all about it after he got back to the room, and he proudly repeated that the promise of a waiver seemed to have done it. Then he looked me in the eye and turned serious again.

"Don't get me wrong," he said. "I'm not insisting on this operation so as to look like some sort of cheap hero. This operation is the only way I can ever recover. If it fails, then I won't have died to no purpose. I'll at least have contributed to medical progress. I'm sure you'd feel the same way. Anyway, I'm just glad it's all settled."

Seeing Shiomi's expression—cheerful yet also inscrutable, as though he were hiding something—I couldn't help feeling somewhat apprehensive. Everyone in the room was deeply concerned, and nobody said another word when it turned out the matter had been decided. Shiomi looked around the silent room, set up his desk on the bed, and lit a cigarette. The winter light was already fading, and you could hear aluminum utensils clattering in the kitchen. Shiomi opened his notebook and just sat there vacantly, his head propped on his left hand.

The day before the operation, Shiomi moved to a room in the surgical ward. After dinner I went to see him there.

As usual he was sitting cross-legged on his bed, looking toward the window and smoking. After my thoracoplasty operation, I myself had had the experience of two weeks in a private room. The single bed and night table felt peaceful and intimate, but the silence was also charged with unpleasant premonitions. Shiomi turned around and smiled when he saw me. His expression conveyed nothing unusual.

"Ryō-chan was here a while ago," he said.

I sat down on the stool by the window.

"What did he want?"

"As always, he wanted me to give up the operation. His arguments were the same as ever: the technique for this type of operation isn't yet advanced enough for it to be safe, it's a big risk even with Dr. Murata, I'm crazy to go ahead with it now, etc. He offered to go straight to Murata and cancel it. He was pretty worked up."

"So what did you say?"

"I told him to mind his own business."

I gave a little laugh.

"You must have had quite a go-around with him."

"No, actually, today he hardly carried on at all. He just said 'I see' and left right away."

I stared vacantly at his burning cigarette. The pale, bluish smoke went floating off lazily toward the bare light bulb hanging from the ceiling.

"So you're really going to do it?"

"Of course. You're not going to get after me like Ryō-chan, are you?"

"Uh-uh. I'm worried, too, though. What if . . ."

"Enough, enough. No what-ifs. I'm not that desperate to live. I'm not like you."

"Me?"

"I'm not joking, you know. You have a strong will to live. I respect that. That's because you're aware of yourself as an artist. An artist *must* live—his life's wasted if he dies without accomplishing anything. Your determination eventually to write something really worthwhile, that's what gives your life meaning. I'm not like that. I once wanted to be an artist, too, but I imagine nearly everybody young feels that way. I wanted to be one even without writing anything, just by observing things. Either that, or I wanted my life to be art. After all, being alive involves giving unique expression to what you are. So that's the way I lived."

"You say you lived like that. Why not say you *live*?"

A long cylinder of ash dropped onto his knee. He looked down and brushed it away with his right hand. Then he brought the cigarette to his lips again and quite unexpectedly released a stream of talk.

"An artist's career is fulfilled in the future, right? His very life depends on what he writes at one time or another, or on what he means to write. A finished work has no value to him, either. His eyes are always on the future—a future that sometimes lies beyond his lifetime. His work then goes forward outside time."

Shiomi paused absently for a drag on his cigarette, which he then dropped into his ashtray, an empty toothpowder can. "However," he went on, "for someone who isn't an artist, life ends on the last of the days he's actually lived. There's no future, only death. Death is the end of everything. There's no present . . . Yes, mostly there isn't even the present, only the past. Obviously, that isn't really living. What other life is there, apart from life *today*? And yet most people live through their past. Their past determines what they are. They're not alive now, they once *were*. Death merely confirms that."

"Don't they say, though, that death transforms life into destiny?"

"That happens too, I suppose. A hero probably dies that way. I'm no hero, though. I've thought about the loneliness of the hero, but I no longer live as I did then."

"That's true of anyone ill."

"Illness has nothing to do with it. Living is something else entirely. It's a kind of intoxication. Everything you have inside you—reason, feeling, knowledge, passion, everything—bursts from you, burning. That's being alive. Come to think of it, I haven't experienced that sort of rapture for a long time. A dizzy rapture, I used to call it. It's gone, though, and I might as well be dead. It means nothing by now if my body happens to die, too."

"Umm . . . aren't you a Christian?"

"Who told you that?" He looked puzzled. "Actually, I used to be interested in Christianity, knew a bit about it, but the more I knew, the more I resisted it. I had to give in in the end, though, and with considerable hesitation I agreed to be baptized. The missionary was such a nice guy, you see, and then . . . Well, there's no point in making excuses. Anyone can have his moment of weakness."

"Do you still have your faith?"

"Oh no. I had a little at the time, that's all. I thought baptism would help me believe. I think I've come through life sincerely enough, but I failed there. You know, though"—he let out a deep sigh—"not too many people get through life without failing somewhere along the line."

The conversation was becoming a bit too gloomy for me. By and large, the evening before an operation should be as cheerful as possible. I said I'd better be going and got up. He stretched out his arm and lit another cigarette.

"Is anyone from your family coming?" I asked, standing by the window.

"No. Just the regular attendant will be good enough for me. Fortunately, the one assigned to me is very nice."

I looked doubtful. He added, "I have no parents, you see. My mother died when I was a child, and my father was killed in an air raid. Back home I have an elder brother, but he's just too busy."

"Surely *someone's* going to come, though?"

For a moment he seemed to stare into the distance. "No, no one," he replied.

Human feelings being what they are, it would be normal to need the care and company of relatives in the period following an operation, and I'd had to assume that his resolve included a willingness to suffer through that painful time alone. Sitting cross-legged there on his bed, dropping the ash from his cigarette into a toothpowder can, he looked very alone indeed.

I was halfway through the door when he called to stop me and remained a moment sunk in thought. "No, I'm not quite sure yet," he said. "Come back tomorrow morning, will you?"

"Of course. Sleep well."

"Thanks. I'm fine."

On the way back to our room, down the dim hallway, I wondered what he had meant. My feet were frozen, and at each brisk step the slap of my sandals echoed along the deserted corridor.

The next morning was bitterly cold. Snow threatened, and our room was dark under the lowering sky. Shiomi's bed, its mattress now bare, looked especially cold.

After breakfast I went to see him in the surgical ward. He was leaning on the windowsill, looking outside, and he turned around when I came in. "It's going to snow today," he said. His breath was white and his lips pale. Still, his expression was perfectly natural and, if anything, cheerful.

"You're certainly taking this in stride."

"Not really." He laughed. "I had a dream last night."

"Tell me."

He thought for a while and then looked me straight in the eye.

"I told you yesterday, didn't I, about this business of 'dizzy rapture.' That's probably where the dream came from. I was walking alone on some mountain, I have no idea where. A warm, violet light shone all around me. Every leaf glittered gold, and in the distance I saw the sea. Then a voice came from the sky. 'On, onward!' it said. It was a clear, childish voice, I don't know whose, and it kept calling to me. There was no one in sight. I did think, though, that I might have heard it before. 'Right, on we go!' I replied. So I strode on. My spirit was washed and clean—I felt truly *séraphique*. The sea came gradually closer. Although alone, I felt as though I were holding hands with everyone I had loved. 'Onward! Further!' the childish voice kept calling, and I kept answering, 'Onward!'"

"And then?"

"Then I woke up. It was daybreak, and light was just coming into the sky. With my eyes open I still felt this indescribable happiness, just as though I'd still been dreaming."

He said no more. I said nothing, either.

"I guess this is my last cigarette," he remarked simply, puffing away with evident pleasure. "It's been a long, long time since I tasted happiness like that. Once, while I was in the army, I was guarding a small village in the Manchurian interior. In spring, the ground everywhere was covered with flowers I couldn't name. I lay down in a meadow and watched clouds just like the ones in Japan. What I was thinking about, I couldn't say. All at once it came to me that I wanted nothing more. I felt as though my life had been well worth living, even if I was to die there and sink into the earth without a thing to mark my grave. I lost track of time."

The nurse came in. "Mr. Shiomi," she said. Then her eyes widened. "Goodness, you're smoking! You mustn't do that!"

"Don't be angry with me. They wouldn't give me any breakfast, and I was desperate."

"It's time for the pre-op exam. Please come to the nurses' office." With this curt speech she bustled off to the next room.

"Time enough when I've finished my cigarette," Shiomi murmured to himself. Then he addressed me in a serious tone.

"Under my pillow," he said, "there are two notebooks."

"Notebooks?"

"Yes, two. The ones I was always writing in. If I don't make it, they're yours."

"What? What are you talking about?"

"Yesterday evening I still wasn't sure, but I think *you*, at least, should be able to understand. Just throw what I've written in the fire if it bores you. I've never in my life had a real friend. While writing I never thought of letting anyone else read it. But you . . . Well, enough. It's just that I've come to believe it'd be all right to let *you* read it. Only if I don't make it, though."

"Don't talk nonsense!" I repeated foolishly.

Shiomi discarded his butt in the usual toothpowder can. "All right," he said, "that's it." We left the room.

Just after noon a nurse wheeled Shiomi on a gurney, dressed in a white hospital gown, from his room to the surgery ward. Kaku and I followed them. Ryō-chan was waiting at a bend in the corridor on the way. His plump body was trembling nervously. Naturally the corridor was freezing cold. There was desolation even in the sound of steam hissing from the pipes. The gurney rolled on until it stopped before the operating room.

Shiomi lay face up on the gurney, with a quilt over him and a towel covering his eyes. He seemed a bit sleepy, having received his first pre-op anesthetic injection upon leaving his room. The nurse accompanying him gave him a second. The door of the operating room opened. We removed the quilt and draped it over a settee in the corridor. Then the nurse rolled the gurney inside.

"Hang in there," I said.

Shiomi moved his lips, probably to murmur that he would be okay. His lips smiled, but his face quickly disappeared behind the closed door. The three of us standing in the corridor heard steam hissing, the clink of scalpels being assembled, and the clattering of the nurses' geta clogs. Then silence fell.

"They've begun," I said. It was five minutes past one.

We went back to our room for the rest period, until three.

We got up again after our temperatures had been taken and saw that a fine snow was falling. The sky was an even gray, and the powdery flakes floated quickly down to the world below. The pine forest outside looked blurred. I suddenly remembered Shiomi saying that morning that it would snow today.

Steam was still hissing from the pipes outside the operating room. They wheeled out a patient who had just undergone thoracoplasty.

"How's it going with Shiomi?" I asked a nurse.

"Mr. Shiomi? Ah, the pneumonectomy. The doctor is having a hard time getting through the pleural adhesions. Still, it seems to be going pretty smoothly."

"Will it take much longer?"

"Oh yes, definitely. It's really only just begun."

The gurney trundled off, and another patient was wheeled in. The corridor was silent again. An old lady who seemed to be the patient's mother asked me with a worried look, "Does it really take that long?"

"Thoracoplasty, you mean? No, no, it'll be over in an hour."

"Really? It's just that all this is new to me, and I'm so worried . . ."

I sat her down on the settee and told her to relax. My own hour of surgery had seemed long enough. No doubt an hour spent waiting is long, but one spent undergoing surgery is worse. The lights went on in the corridor, and I paced up and down it. At last the other patient's operation was over, and out he came. His mother thanked me and went off after the gurney.

"How's Shiomi?" I asked the nurse.

"At this rate he'll be fine. His blood pressure is hardly down at all."

She hurried back into the operating room. After a moment's thought I returned to my room. It was dinnertime. Everyone gave me worried looks, and we began an interminable round of desultory talk. I ate my cold soup. More and more snow kept falling, there in the semi-darkness outside the window. After dinner, Ryō-chan and I went off again to the surgery wing. The corridor was quieter than ever. All you could hear was the occasional scrape of one scalpel against another. There were two operating tables, and work on the one devoted to thoracoplasty seemed to be over for the day. It certainly was taking a long time.

"I really should have persuaded him to give it up," Ryō-chan said abruptly.

"It's a bit late for that."

"I'm getting really worried. Yesterday evening I kept telling him to cancel it . . ."

Ryō-chan sat down on the settee and went on fidgeting. His usually rosy face was almost purple with cold. I wasn't feeling too confident either. I kept wishing the operation would be over. All of a sudden the door opened, and a nurse rushed out.

"What's happened?" we both asked, rising.

"We're giving him a transfusion. He's all right. The upper lobe should be out soon."

She ran off and returned carrying the kettle reserved for operating room use. "Apparently he's taking out the lower lobe, too," she said and rushed back in.

"What? The lower lobe, too?" Ryō-chan asked breathlessly, but the door was already shut.

Ryō-chan turned toward me with a somber look on his face. "He's finished," he said, spitting out the words. We then lapsed back into silence, straining our ears for any sound in the operating room.

"It's turning into a real blizzard," Kaku remarked as he came up and stood in silence beside us. Our faces probably looked angry. The cold grew as the night wore on. Sometimes I paced the corridor just to warm up my numb feet. "I put in a foot-warmer for him," Kaku told me abruptly.

Nine o'clock came and went. Lights-out was at nine.

"Go back to the room," I said. "I'll wait a little longer to see how things go."

Ryō-chan went right away. Kaku stayed till about ten. "I'll see you," he said and left. Struggling against mounting anxiety, I sat down on the settee and rubbed my hands together. There was not a soul in the corridor. The doctor on night duty passed by once, with a suspicious glance at me, on his way to the physicians' office. From the brightly lit operating room came now and again the scrape of a scalpel or a low voice.

It was a long wait. I walked to the very end of the corridor and looked out through the window into the gloom of the garden. It was still snowing, and the nandina bushes wore rounded masses of snow. Dead silence reigned in the patients' wing, and the only light was in the nurses' office. I pressed my face against the icy glass, murmuring over and over, "Please, please!"

Back I went to the operating room. I wasn't at all sleepy. Instead, anxiety made it difficult to breathe, and I felt nauseous. I bent over and pressed my shaking hands to my mouth. Eleven o'clock, too, went by. I felt as though I must be dreaming.

In the operating room there was a sudden commotion. I rose unsteadily to my feet and went to stand outside the door. I heard sounds of turmoil. The doctor's voice was sharp, scolding. Then silence. I leaned weakly against the door. It opened, and the head surgical nurse emerged. She peered hesitantly into my face when she saw me. Her lips seemed to tremble. "He didn't make it," she said.

A nightmare. That's how it came at me, as a nightmare. The pale, exhausted face of this nurse who otherwise always smiled, the dim lighting of the deserted corridor, the hissing of steam, and I myself, on vigil there—everything was wrong. "Intraoperative decease at eleven thirty-five P.M.," she added, as though reciting a catechism.

The nurse and I wheeled the gurney to the private room in the surgical ward. Shiomi's face looked exactly as though he were still under the anesthetic. This was no sleeping face, though. The smell of what he'd called this morning his last cigarette still lingered faintly in the room, like incense.

With heavy steps I trod the passageway back to my room. Drifted snow lined one side of it, gleaming faintly. To avoid it I kept to the other side, but even so I heard snow crunch now and again under my sandals. Every room in the general admissions ward was dark and silent except mine, where a desk lamp shed a faint light into the corridor. It was Kaku's. I opened the door, and Kaku, who till a moment ago had apparently been reading, sat up abruptly. Ryō-chan, the young fellow by the window, and Pop all sat up, too.

I sat down on my bed and wrapped my feet in the quilt. Their collective gaze bored into me so sharply that it hurt.

"He didn't make it." I stopped there. No one said a word. The soft whisper of the falling snow only deepened the silence.

"They got the upper lobe out all right." I passed on what the nurse had told me. "The lesions in the lower lobe were worse than expected, though, and Dr. Murata asked him what he should do. He said to go ahead. But the adhesions were so bad, Murata recommended giving up."

I stopped talking. I was having trouble breathing. Everyone waited, perfectly still. "Then Shiomi apparently told Murata loud and clear that, as far as he was concerned, Murata should go on. So Murata did, and he got the lower lobe out as well. In the end, they were just sewing him up again when his blood pressure suddenly dropped. It seems he'd already had two transfusions, you see . . ." I said no more.

"The idiot!" Ryō-chan shouted. "The damned idiot!" It was almost a shriek. "I *told* him to give it up! I don't know *how* many times I told him!"

There on his bed Ryō-chan wept, his plump body shaking. By the lamp's dim light he wept on and on. The rest of us hung our heads, as though charged with some grave offense. Outside in the woods, snow now and again slid off a branch with a thump.

The weather the next morning was glorious. Sunlight glittered from every snow-covered branch. The snow on the ground was over a foot deep. The stronger of the patients went out into the garden with happy cries. The dripping from the roof to the south grew louder and louder. Sparrows were cheeping everywhere.

We accompanied Shiomi's body to the mortuary. Ours were the first footprints on the path through the woods. The sunlight filtering through the branches dappled the pristine snow. Sometimes cold drops fell from high branches onto our heads.

There was to be a postmortem. We had nothing more to do until the wake that night. We put his photograph up in front of the altar and returned to the patients' wing. It was then that I remembered the notebooks Shiomi had mentioned.

Under the quilt in that chilly private room lay two harmless-looking, medium-sized notebooks. I put them under my arm and asked the nurse to tidy up the quilt and have it disinfected. Shiomi's brother wouldn't arrive from their home until late that night or early the next morning. Apart from the quilt there were practically no other possessions to look after.

Once again I followed the path to the mortuary. The sun grew brighter and brighter, and the snow more dazzlingly white. On tree trunks I knocked out the snow that caught between the teeth of my geta. The dry sound echoed into the distance.

Wasn't that suicide? The question pursued me obstinately. Shiomi had volunteered for the operation, and during it he'd consistently asked the surgeon to see it through. He undoubtedly knew that it was dangerous and that for someone in his weakened condition it could be fatal. What if I'd adamantly opposed it? Beyond such regrets as these, however, it soothed my sense of powerlessness somewhat to realize that his stubborn will would probably have overcome any objections. Mingled with these regrets, though, there was still that initial suspicion. Hadn't that operation been for Shiomi, baptized as he was, a way of deliberately killing himself? The question tore at my heart amid the brilliant sunlight and the answering white dazzle of the snow.

Seated on the cold tatami of the mortuary, with snowmelt endlessly pattering around me, I plunged into reading Shiomi Shigeshi's two notebooks.

The First Notebook

Death comes to us all, and one day I, too, will die. For me, that's just a given. But there's no way to know when it will happen, so people just drift along from day to day. They never actually realize they're alive and waste all the time they have. The future being hazy, they feel no fear or anything much else. It's different for someone like me, though, someone who knows that when his time is up his body will grow cold and gradually merge with wind and rain and earth. I'm going to die. I really am. And my time, the time I have to live, is probably very short.

Does the dreamer really have no memory of having dreamed? In childhood I often had nightmares. I'd wake up (in my dream), clutching the rumpled bedclothes, to find myself alone in a small, closed room with a putrid smell in the air. It was so dark I couldn't see my own fingers, but I could feel the ceiling and the walls slowly closing in on me. Down came the ceiling, inch by inch, while the walls squeezed in toward me, soon to crush me to bits. That's when I'd really wake up, screaming. There I'd be in my room, as usual, on my own bed. My relief wouldn't last, though, because the ceiling would still be inching down toward me, while the walls grew thicker and thicker, and I desperately wondered why. This *couldn't* be a dream, because I'd definitely woken up just now. Any minute I'd be squashed as flat as a dried squid, I really would. This was it. There was no escape. I'd scream, and this time I'd wake up for real. But even then, who could guarantee that I wasn't still dreaming?

This happened several times. I was a small, scruffy, timid boy. As time went by I lost track of what these nightmares really meant. Eventually I went into the army and compromised my health. After being discharged I got a job, but my health meanwhile deteriorated beyond recall. Until I entered the sanatorium, though, and saw scientific proof of my condition, the death that awaits us all didn't frighten me much, despite my being *mortel* like anyone else.

This is a dream, I told myself when I first heard the doctor's verdict. It won't last. When I wake up again I'll just be able to dismiss it. After all, this life of mine is a gift, isn't it, good for one time only? And life is far more special than this—brighter, more worthwhile, more *brillant*. Those were my thoughts at the time. I never woke up, though. In the end I had to recognize that I'd never wake up till the day I died, and that this nightmarish dread would be my only reality. When I open my eyes tomorrow morning I'll have my old health back; the smell of cresol, the hospital gown's rough texture, the unpleasant cough, the slight, nasty fever will all be gone, and I'll be able to step out gaily into the bustling city—is there a sick man anywhere who doesn't indulge in these pointless fancies? I'm not dreaming, though. The X-ray photos, the Gaffky readings are no dream. Never again will I be free to wander about as I please. A man this ill is certain to die before long. This reality—the sole reality now available to me—is the only life I've been given. After a long period of self-delusion, that's the unpleasant truth I've had to accept. I'll never wake up till I die, which is bound to happen soon. My experience of life doesn't deserve to be called living. My thirty years—college till graduation, then a job for a while, then the army, and finally this sanatorium—have run their dreary, futile course. I can neither change the past nor embrace the future. I have no present or future, only a past. How, then, can I really live at all? How can I get a conscious grip on a life that's just drifting away?

That's the state of mind I reached in the end. At least in Japanese, the expression "state of mind" suggests a very Eastern sort of tranquility, like that of still water, but my état d'âme was more a raging torrent. An indescribable despair tormented me, and I wavered helplessly between pent-up anger and bouts of numb resignation. I even sought refuge for a time in Christianity. Remembering that a girl I once loved had loved God more than any man, I who loved no one in the world struggled to love God and put myself entirely in his hands. However, God never revealed himself to me. No doubt he disapproved all too naturally of my excessive desires and my arrogant inability to love even myself. Then came darkness. After seeking a while to cling to God I felt sorry for myself and hated him. I had nothing left, nothing at all. Even my courage, which should have supported me, just weighed on me like a yoke.

I wasn't in the least afraid of death. Well, no, I'd probably be exaggerating if I said I didn't fear it at all, but most of my anxiety came instead from dissatisfaction with life. I'd always been solitary. The people I loved left me. While I loved them, though, I was alive, I felt fulfilled, and a sort of dizzy rapture swept over me. Where did that happiness go? Ah, that burning, spiritual joy, so consuming I could have cried out—where did it go? Solitude permeated by a stubborn will, a hero's solitude, and then this maudlin, pitiful aloneness that overwhelmed me in daily life—what was it all about? Once I was a callow, ignorant youth exploring the labyrinth of life, but at least my heart was full of yearning, and life seemed worth living. I even aspired to beauty of spirit. How different I was then! At eighteen I knew love, and now I have no love at all. At twenty-four I knew desire, and now I desire no one. Once I was alive, and now life is gone from me.

Is this really true, though? Was I really then so brilliantly alive? I who never successfully inspired love was content just to love, yet secret suffering still rent my heart. Was there really nothing about my life to regret? And then there's that other question. Why did the people I loved leave me? Where did I go wrong? I dealt honestly with them. I never hurt them. If I was the one to get hurt, that's only because I was spiritually weak and delicate. Or so I tell myself. But is it true? Did I really never go astray?

So I decided to stop brooding pointlessly over the present and to turn my gaze toward the past. I wanted to retrace my past footsteps and so live again in the present. A return to the realm of memory might seem to be an evasion, an escape from the present; but for someone like me, who could never renew his life and whose every day was so restricted, what other life of my own was possible, beside reliving the past? Having come through youth without regret, I could continue my journey toward death in the same spirit. If I could say yes to my life, I could also say yes to my death and choose death freely, as Nietzsche put it. I might even be able to solve the mystery that so far had always defeated me—that of love—and so die with a smile on my lips.

I decided to go ahead. The other patients' babble no longer reached me when I did so. The nurses' white uniforms, the bed-clothes reeking of medications, the fear of death—everything vanished. I was alone. In the world of memories I can roam as I please. Remembering is living. For the first time since I learned I was ill, the attitude that had been mine until then—shut up inside myself, struggling in vain against a despair of my own creation—came to seem pathetic. I laughed. I laughed loudly enough to startle the others.

Forward, then. But conscious effort to remember can easily go wrong. The only way to grasp again vague impressions of the past is to write them down and fix them, dispassionately. So I went to the sanatorium store and bought these two plain notebooks, and this is what I've written in them so far. I'll now focus on two passages of my youth, the spring of my eighteenth year and the autumn of my twenty-fourth, and recreate each as truthfully as I can. In both I loved someone with all my heart. Nonetheless, the mystery of love remained for me complete. Whether I can resolve it now, I don't know. I'll be glad enough if just scribbling can get me through each day, till I die, in full freedom of spirit. I haven't ever written much, and I'm not doing this for anyone else to read.

I may not write well, but I mean to convey in these notebooks, as carefully as I can, the young man that I was then.

The wind against my cheeks carried the damp chill of a spring morning. The vapor rising from the sea lingered here and there like smoke, but it vanished once the boat left the harbor and raced over mounting waves across the bright blue sea. The pipe sticking up by the engine room let out two bursts of white steam, and sharp whistles rang out over the smooth water. The deck smelled of fish. I sat down in the stern and gazed ahead. The sea breeze stung my eyes, somewhat heavy as they still were with sleep.

Tachibana and I were alone in the stern. Before us stood the wooden engine-room housing, gray from exposure to the salt air. Along the narrow passageway south of it my classmates leaned against the railing, sunning themselves, shoulder to shoulder with the upperclassmen. The wind brought us their laughing voices over the creels and cargo scattered about the deck, and the seated figures of people who looked like traveling salesmen. We couldn't see the first-year students from where we were—they must have clustered together in the bow. Tachibana and I both had paperbacks open on our laps, as though to say we had no time for small talk, but the chugging engine sent such vibrations through me that the print, which didn't really absorb me that much anyway, seemed to dance before my eyes. Now and again I'd lift my gaze to the sea.

I shouldn't really be aboard this chugging boat at all now, I reminded myself. I should be hiking with Fujiki over the mountains from Shuzenji. We'd have followed the Katsura River for a while, then struck off on a mountain trail that took us so high we'd hear larks singing below us. Finally, from the top of Daruma Pass, we'd have looked down on Heda Bay, shining in the sun. That dream of crossing the pass alone with Fujiki had come to nothing, like all my others. Still, I couldn't help thinking that my own foolishness was to blame.

Who cares, though, I told myself, if I'm a fool. I stood up, feeling Tachibana's stare boring into my back. No doubt he felt sorry for me. I realized when I started walking that the swell was bigger than I'd thought. I lurched forward, clinging to the steel railing, as far as the passageway past the engine room.

A row of impassive faces announced that the scenery had lost its charm. Hattori and Yanai were deep in conversation. Seated next to them Kinoshita, who had slept the whole way on the train, was again drowsing away. One of the upperclassmen called out to me not to fall.

I got past the engine room, and all at once my eyes took in the bow, the sea, and, to port, the Izu coast. Four or five first-year students sat in a circle in the bow, catching all the wind. Half a dozen more leaned against the railing nearby, watching the sea. Fujiki was in the circle. Yashiro, next to him, spotted me coming and half stood up to wave, but the launch rolled, and he nearly fell onto Fujiki's shoulder. Yashiro hooted with laughter, but Fujiki was looking down, and I couldn't make out his expression. With growing nervousness I staggered over to him.

"The wind's cold here, isn't it?" I remarked as I sat down.

I sat there and blew into my numb hands. Right behind Yashiro, I was out of the wind from the head down, and the sun was warm.

Next to me, Fujiki's cape billowed and flapped loudly in the wind. He looked at me.

Fujiki's eyes—those two black eyes of his always held me spellbound. Impossibly clear, coldly luminous as crystal, they pierced me through in an instant, and my heart seemed to falter each time, as though I were about to be reborn with new beauty. Those eyes were definitely telling me something, but, alas, I couldn't make out what it was. Fujiki looked down again.

"That's Mito over there, isn't it, Shiomi?" Yashiro asked.

The boat didn't go directly from Numazu to Cape Ose but instead hugged the coast. Right now we were off Enoura Bay.

"I don't think so, not yet. As I remember, last year the boat put in somewhere on the way—Mito, I think it was."

"It's about an hour to Heda?"

"Right, about an hour."

Yashiro looked at his watch. Sunlight glinted off the glass.

"Feels good, doesn't it, Fujiki?" I peered at him.

He said nothing. We were now pitching wildly. Actually, it didn't feel that good at all. The prow bit into the deep blue, green-striped water, and the center of gravity tipped forward till the boat threatened to go straight down. Surging water filled our entire field of vision, as though at any moment we might vanish beneath the waves. But then the gleaming whitecaps would part, the vessel would regain its balance, and the waves raced by on either side in many colors, from white to pale blue, green, purple, or ultramarine, and stippled between the stripes with countless little eddies. This went on and on. You felt your chest tighten as though death were calling.

"Those colors look good enough to eat," Mori remarked. "They remind me of Aoki-dō's custard pudding."

"The ones in the waves, you mean?" This was Ishii.

"Right."

"How vulgar can you get!"

"Nice colors, though. They make you want to dive right into them."

"Come off it! Only Shiomi could get away with sounding that romantic!"

Mori looked put out. Yashiro and Ishii both laughed. Fujiki, his cape collar up, still had his head bent over.

"You okay, Fujiki?" I asked.

He raised his head and looked directly at me with big, moist eyes full of lonely entreaty, eyes seeming to expect sympathy and protection. His face, though, was expressionless. Silently he shook his head from side to side, then dropped it again. The wind stirred the close-cropped hair, a bit long now, that stuck out from under his cap at the nape of his neck.

I stood up and made my way back past the engine room to Tachibana.

"We're coming into Mito now?" I asked pointlessly.

Tachibana glanced up from his book and gave me a puzzled look. "I dunno," he answered gruffly. "Probably won't stop there at all unless some passenger wants to get off."

I sat down beside him, and the strain I'd just experienced, the dry tension in the throat, melted away. The boat was forging straight ahead, giving Mito a wide berth. To starboard, a gentle spring mist floated about the horizon, with Mount Fuji soaring lightly above it. The blotches visible here and there must be seagulls. A white wake surged endlessly from the stern, like a trail of tossing funeral bouquets, to die away in the distance.

All right! I always felt at peace, reading a book like this next to Tachibana. I'd shared a dormitory room with him for two years now, and we were completely at ease with each other. What could have gotten into me, to make me attempt a nervous approach to Fujiki, a first-year student, and sound out his feelings? Why on earth had I gone staggering along the deck for a look at his face? I should have stayed right here. I should have stayed put next to Tachibana, breathing in the salt wind with its faint tang of regret . . . But my gloomy preoccupation soon roused a welter of memories and the romantic fantasies that colored them. I forgot all about my book. The wind blew it off my lap.

Things were livening up on deck. We'd passed Cape Ose and were sliding in close past cliffs of alternating red earth and jutting black rock. Swept up by the hubbub of voices, I joined the others along the port railing. The spray from the waves breaking against the cliffs almost rebounded on us. Suddenly the launch leaned steeply to port, and the whistle blew shrilly. A long, pine-clad promontory appeared to starboard, where a moment ago there had been only boundless ocean. The waves became smooth, and the noise of the engine dropped. We were coming into Heda Bay. There beneath the pines stood the familiar black college dormitory roof, the brownish jetty, the drab houses, then slopes covered with tangerine orchards, and Daruma Pass. As I took stock of it all, the boat meanwhile glided swiftly up to the village wharf at the back of the deeply recessed harbor.

It was about a mile and a half to the college lodge. The narrow, stone-paved path, smelling of fish, followed the shore of the bay in a gentle curve. We disembarked and set off along it in twos and threes.

I walked with Tachibana. In my heart of hearts I'd have preferred to slow down and drop back to join the others behind us, but I wanted no more of Tachibana's ironic looks. In the end, though, I just couldn't help turning to glance back.

"It hasn't changed a bit since last year, has it?" Tachibana remarked.

"It's so peaceful," I chimed in.

To our right, on the sunlit veranda of a fisherman's shabby house, a boy watched us pass with wondering eyes, his head wrapped in bandages. The buds on a cherry tree in the scrap of a garden were swelling, but it would be some time yet before they bloomed. On the side away from us the garden ended at a rock wall, beyond which stretched the blue waters of the bay.

"It must have been pretty cold here this year," I said. "I'd say that cherry tree's late."

"No. Last year was about the same. In our first year we just didn't feel it, we were so nervous about the winter training session. This year we'll probably be slacking off a bit."

"I don't know. The cold just went on and on. I remember it was freezing the day we got our exam results."

"Nonsense! We were just shivering because we were afraid we'd failed!"

Tachibana laughed, and I caught his good cheer. He began talking.

"You probably didn't realize because you're in humanities, but in math our grades were so low we had a terrible time. Yanai, Kinoshita, and I—all borderline cases—actually went to see the head math teacher to put in our plea for favorable consideration. It was a dark night and, believe me, it was cold. The shakiest among us was Yanai, who'd been warned about his grades in both the first and second semesters. I'd had a warning in the first. That's the way it goes, I suppose—one battle after another."

"Kinoshita must have been all right, though?"

"Kinoshita, yes, he more or less gets by, so he came along to support us. The three of us were pretty nervous. There we were, in front of his brazier, and he told us to go ahead and warm up, so Yanai put his hands out over it. His voice shook, though, it was so cold. Actually, it was pretty funny. Finally, just when he was rounding off his speech, he stuck his face over the brazier and snot dropped from his nose onto the coals below. There was a big hiss."

"You must have laughed."

"We certainly did. We cracked up and just kept laughing, it was so funny. Yanai got angry."

"Did the head teacher laugh, too?"

"You could tell he wanted to, but he made a funny face instead and stopped himself. He really gave us a piece of his mind, though. He said he didn't grade hard, he'd even given full marks to one of the first year students, and so on."

"Right," I blurted out, "he must have meant Fujiki." Fujiki was the top science student.

"Yes, Fujiki's good. Anyway, we were all lucky he didn't fail us. It's almost a miracle that Yanai didn't fail."

"Founder's Day is the problem. You get into the habit of drinking on Founder's Day, and you end up slacking off all the way to the exams. And next year there'll be the college entrance exams. Maybe all the science students will end up having to take them over."

"Don't tempt fate!" Tachibana laughed.

The fishy-smelling, stone-paved path curved toward the right, and we passed the last house. Immediately to our right was the sea, and to our left a cliff of bare, red earth. There seemed to be some sort of work going on, because sand-filled buckets were moving up and down on a motor-driven mechanism.

"Slowpokes!"

Someone had hailed us from behind. I turned to see Mori and Ishii pass us briskly while we gazed up at the top of the cliff.

"Fujiki's fine, Shiomi." Mori spoke rapidly. "There's nothing to worry about."

Lanky Ishii, suitcase in hand, and chubby Mori, trotting along beside him, drew steadily ahead of us. For a while we could still hear Ishii talking.

"The Greeks, you see, had faith in Man. At first they had faith in the gods, then they had faith in Man, who'd created the gods, and finally they had faith in the laws, arts, and philosophy that Man had created. The Greeks strove above all for the greatest possible humanity. Their gods are models of human beauty. Even that solemn Plato . . ."

Plato, eh? That had to be a dig at me. Fujiki's wan face floated before me.

When the boat reached the wharf the liveliest of us had disembarked first, while I'd plopped down on a rope-wrapped stanchion at the wharf's edge, as though exhausted, to wait for Fujiki. He'd been deathly pale when he reached the side of the boat, accompanied by Yashiro. A three- or four-foot gap separated the boat from the wharf, which was a little lower. "Can you jump that?" Yashiro asked. Fujiki flushed, and jumped. By the time I rose to my feet he was standing unsteadily on the wharf. Ishii came up as though to support him. "Here, Fujiki," I said, "sit here and take a rest." Fujiki's smile of thanks froze. He sat down, looking glum, as Yashiro came behind him, both hands loaded with baggage. I started away. "Fujiki's not much of a sailor, Shiomi," Mori informed me. "No," I replied, "he isn't tough, like you!" I'd walked off across the wharf without looking back.

The height of the cliff to our left had lessened, and the pinewood on that side was now at our level. On the right, a sandy beach stretched between us and the sea. The morning sun glinted peacefully on the waters of the bay. We quickened our pace to get through the pines and came out beside the silent, still-shuttered buildings. In the quadrangle Yanai, our Captain, had his arms spread out like a traffic policeman.

"The place is all ours this year," he was saying. "This way! Let's get the second-floor room on the south! Move in, move right in!"

Tachibana and I mounted the dim stairway to the second floor. The large, eight-mat room smelled of mold. Hattori had thrown the window open and was seated on the frame, looking out at the sea. Kinoshita, in the middle of the room, held an open notebook.

"What's this?" Tachibana inquired. "Already doing the accounts?"

"No, no," Hattori explained, "he's just too hungry to move."

I went up to the window, took off my jacket, and filled my lungs with the salty breeze. Sudden happiness filled me. Yes, I said to myself, I'm glad I came! Down below, you could hear Yanal barking orders.

"We'll be eating right away, so put your luggage down and go straight to the dining room. We all have work to do this afternoon."

I came down the stairs last, soap case in hand. There was a washbasin along the concrete passageway between our building and the next. I worked the pump handle, and water poured into the old metal basin. Through the window I suddenly spotted Fujiki coming down the path through the pines, two or three paces behind Yashiro. He seemed to be making hard work of carrying a small bag, but his cheeks were rosy. My heart beat fast, and I plunged my face vigorously into the cold water.

Heda is a small fishing village the west coast of the Izu Peninsula. A long, slender promontory and barren cliffs dominate the entrance to a dreary bay where oil slicks wander the waves, shrinking and spreading. During the day the fire tower, the elementary school, the village office, the post office, a pair of inns, and the roofs of low, sea-front fishermen's houses stretch away to either side of the main wharf at the back of the harbor, while beneath a reddish-brown bluff the ruin of a late Tokugawa-period shipyard building, and the bare skeleton of a wooden ship, cast their quiet shadows over the bay. At night, phosphorescent creatures gleam silver in the wake of boats, around wharf pilings, and in the seaweed washed up on the shore.

I haven't been back there for over ten years. That run-down village must still be drowsing away, though, there at the edge of the sea. It's a hard place to get to, whether you take the motor launch—the "chug-chug"—from Numazu or walk the twelve miles over Daruma Pass from Shuzenji, and no scenic spots or historic monuments draw the traveler there in the first place. Only in summer do students crowd into the college lodge there and turn the place into a lively swimming resort for young men. The oars of the local boats leave lazily spreading rings among the ripples of the bay, and red loincloths flash from the diving board. In front of the village's one sweet shop, Akizuki, college students munch their bean-jam buns with a disgruntled air. Once summer is over, though, only scruffy fishermen's children roam the breakwater, barefoot in the cold autumn wind, as though it were all theirs. In winter the place is quieter still.

Heda in spring: what *we* knew was Heda in the two weeks from March into April, when the cherries on the point were in bloom. My high school archery club normally got together in the college lodge there at the end of the school year. Most of the rest of the time we were caught up in a series of contests, and during practice sessions the upperclassmen's constant carping about our form or accuracy made us feel small. At this spring get-together, though, we all fell under the blossoms' spell, and you didn't have to worry even if you missed the target completely. Most high school sports are a succession of matches and meets, which doesn't leave much room for actually enjoying them, but at these Heda gatherings we could have as much cheeky fun with archery as we pleased.

Besides, we were all very young. That year was my eighteenth, and my second in high school. The obnoxious third-years had all graduated, those who'd passed their college entrance exams were feeling fine, those who'd failed looked crestfallen, and all in all there was nothing in the world to be afraid of. Most of the first-year students were quiet enough. One or two were a good deal older than me, having been held back repeatedly, but they bowed to an upperclassman's authority. There were twenty of us altogether, including the former club members—now at university—who'd joined us. In the morning and the afternoon we did archery, then played cards and carom late into the night. We never got tired. We loved our discussions, too. Curious about everything, we never conceded a point until fully convinced. Our hearts were fresh, and our joys and sorrows untainted.

Morning and afternoon we practiced archery by turns in groups of three.

The lodge buildings stood around a quadrangle in the middle of the promontory, sheltered from the sea wind by windbreak trees. The sessions were held on a long, narrow plot of open ground behind the lodge complex. That first afternoon we'd all pitched in to set up a makeshift archery range. We spread mats at the closer end, and at the far end we piled earth into a rudimentary target mound with a row of three targets on it, each two feet wide. That was all. The mound was so low that any misdirected arrow would fly straight over it and lose itself in the weeds beyond. "Great!" the shout would go up. "A home run for Yanai!" Then some of us would go looking for the arrow, which could take quite a while. Anyway, three shot their arrows together, so your turn didn't come around that often. While waiting you could lean against the breakwater of big, round, heaped-up boulders, walk about on it, or even cross it to stroll around on the beach. Leaning on the breakwater that way, we looked more than anything else like seals sunning themselves at the zoo. When your turn came your Japanese dress, with its *hakama* trousers, made you look like a bird.

I felt sleepy there in the warm sun, sheltered from the wind. The cherry trees were coming at last into bloom, against the background of the pinewood. The *kasuri* splash patterns of the kimono, the black full-skirted *hakama*, each archer's single shoulder bared to the white undergarment, and the very bows flickered and glittered. Even the twang of the bowstrings sounded like the lazy droning of bees.

A sudden movement.

"What are you thinking about, Shiomi, here all on your own?"

That insinuating voice coming my way, a teasing, slightly mocking purr—it had to be Yashiro. He was a year older than me, having been held back because he'd failed his high school entrance exam the year before. I was the upperclassman, though, so he spoke rather more politely than he might have done otherwise.

"I'm not thinking about anything," I answered dully.

"You always seem to be taking off by yourself. It'd be nice if you joined us over there and gave up hanging about in the wilds. Even Fujiki . . ."

"I'm fine here," I replied hastily.

"Actually, Shiomi, you're being a bit of a coward. You've got to talk to Fujiki more and spend time with him. The way you keep skulking around in the background just makes him uncomfortable, you know. He said a while ago he feels as though you're always spying on him."

I half turned away and ran my hand over the big boulder I'd just been leaning against. It was smooth and faintly warm.

"I'm a coward, all right," I protested, "but Fujiki's even worse than I am. In my experience . . ."

"I don't want to know about your experience."

Yashiro flashed a broad smile that made him look grown-up and ever so shrewd. "Anyway," he added officiously, "he's still a child. He doesn't understand things."

I pretended not to know what he was talking about. Nonetheless, from my distance at the breakwater my eyes never missed Fujiki moving about or stopping with downcast eyes, or making the slightest movement of any kind. I simply couldn't take my eyes off him as long as I was anywhere near him. Fujiki's mere existence intoxicated me, like a warm spring wind.

Yashiro's suddenly lowered voice brought me back to my senses.

"Whatever happened to that business of hiking over Daruma Pass? When we all got together at Tokyo Station you and Fujiki were supposed to be on your way there already, and I was meaning to ask about you."

"It fell through."

"Why? You'd been planning it so carefully. And you looked so happy. You even told *me* about it!"

"It fell through because Fujiki said he'd rather go with everyone else on the launch."

"But why? I just don't understand." Yashiro wouldn't give up. "I've tried asking him, but he won't answer."

So Fujiki hadn't given Yashiro any reason. That, at least, struck me as a sign of goodwill. Come to think of it, though, what *was* the reason? *Why* hadn't Fujiki agreed to hike over the pass with me?

I moved away from the breakwater. I'd had enough of Yashiro sticking his nose into my secret. Perhaps everyone knew about it already, but I still preferred to keep it to myself. I wanted the secret of my feeling for Fujiki left alone, without any meddling from anyone. I'd been a fool, no doubt about it, to let the hiking plan slip to Yashiro.

"I want to be alone," I told Yashiro when he came after me.

I threaded my way through the cherry trees to where Kinoshita was supervising the practice and keeping score. Yashiro gave up and went back to join the other seals on the breakwater.

Every tree trunk had several bows leaned against it, and archery gloves hung from the branches. On the sidelines I tried a few bows till I found one I liked, tucked it under my arm, and slipped my own glove onto my right hand. My turn was coming up. From the quiver I took four of my arrows, then peeled my outer jacket off one shoulder. I was ready. Three of us, when our names were called, removed our geta and stepped onto the mat spread on the ground. Our senior, a college student, strolled up beside Kinoshita and stood there to watch us, cigarette in hand.

I half knelt on the mat, one knee up, and looked toward the target. I was beginning to feel better. Glancing toward the target, I pressed my thumb to the tip of my ring finger and rubbed the two together. Then I turned to face forward, slowly picked up the bow, and fixed my gaze on the target. I put more strength into my bow hand and unhurriedly drew back the string. Silence reigned. I let fly. The string twanged . . . and the arrow missed and went some way behind the target.

"You're still rushing it, Shiomi," Kasuga, the college student, remarked from the side.

I paused as form required, brought the bow around in front of me, and returned to the half-kneeling position, one knee up. Kasuga watched me with a friendly smile on his face.

"It's no good," I said. "I just can't hold out till the right moment."

The smoke from his cigarette trailed off, to vanish among the cherry trees. I fitted another arrow to the string, stood up, looked at the target, brought the bow into position, reminding myself not to release too soon—oh, I knew the theory of it well enough. Then I drew the bow all the way and held it there with every ounce of my strength, so that at any moment the arrow might fly. With mounting concentration I awaited the impending discharge. It was like meditation. All at once the string rang in my ears, and instantly there came the thwack of the arrow piercing the target. "Still way off!" a voice called from over by the mound,

"Nope!" Kasuga announced the bitter truth.

"I *did* hit the target, though."

"You just don't have it together with your bow. So you hit the target—who cares? You're going into third year, and you have a big responsibility. How long are you going to go on with hits like that?"

"I suppose it's nerves," I said, "releasing like that too soon."

"That's right." He assumed a medical student's knowing expression. "Your nerves are shot. You're spirit's sick."

"All right, but then why did I hit the target at all? Maybe I'd do better not to."

"The goal of archery isn't to hit the target, you know. The pleasure of it must be simply in drawing the bow. When you're rushing it, then throughout the process, from the time you hold the bow erect until the arrow strikes, your desire to hit the target takes precedence over that pleasure. That desire's your problem. Your spirit just isn't with you, you see. Instead, it rushes off to the target as soon as you start to hold up the bow. That shows there's no spirit in your bow."

Time for the next arrow, and again I drew a spiritless bow. The arrow hit the center of the bull's-eye.

"You see," Kasuga went on, "you're neurotic, which means that your spirit wants to go wandering off elsewhere. Your body is here, but not your spirit. Don't worry too much, though. Everyone has times like that."

For the sake of appearances I shot my fourth arrow. Then I bowed, stepped off the mat, leaned the bow against the trunk of a cherry tree, unfastened my archery glove, and hung it on a branch. That done, I walked with Kasuga and the two others to rejoin the group at the breakwater. My spirit is elsewhere, I kept whispering to myself.

I got off at the suburban railway station and left the bright shopping street lights to walk over the level crossing. From there the road was dark and empty. I strode along briskly, clutching in one hand the book I'd been reading and a folded map. Then I caught the sweet, penetrating fragrance of daphne. Where it was coming from I couldn't tell, but it stirred hopeful fancies in me. Suddenly I felt as though all would be well, and happiness swelled within me. Each step I took rang out louder than the last.

Fujiki's house wasn't that far from the station. The light over the door dimly illuminated his name-card, Fujiki Shinobu, stuck up beside the entrance in lieu of a regular nameplate. Having come that far I hesitated a moment, then resolutely opened the lattice door. The bell attached to the door jingled loudly as usual.

Standing there in the darkened entrance, I was about to announce my presence when the sliding panel into the next room opened and light flooded in. Against the light a girl wearing a red sweater over her sailor uniform came almost dancing out toward me.

"Goodness, it's Mr. Shiomi!" she exclaimed happily and turned back to announce loudly to her brother, "Mr. Shiomi's here!" The next moment she invited me in.

A small desk in the middle of the eight-mat room was covered with textbooks and notebooks. Before a somewhat larger desk that faced away from the tokonoma, at a right angle to the latticework window in the hall, sat Fujiki himself, looking serious. In front of him lay a closely printed book in a foreign language. He nodded slightly when he saw me but made no move to get up.

The girl, who'd been struggling to suppress her merriment, now went to the closet and took out a cushion that she placed before the small desk in the middle of the room. After seating me on it she bowed very politely, hands to the floor, and bade me welcome.

"Where's your mother?" I asked.

"Do excuse me, Mr. Shiomi," a bright, youthful voice answered from the kitchen. "I'm doing some tidying up."

"It's all right, Mother," the girl stepped in to assure her. Then to me she went on, "You see, I have a favor to ask."

"Oh, Chie-chan, you mustn't."

"It's all right, Mother, you keep out of it. You don't mind, Mr. Shiomi, do you?"

"I have no idea what you want, Chie, but of course I'll do whatever you ask."

The girl looked at me coaxingly, with big eyes.

"The year-end exams are coming soon, right? I'd really appreciate it if you'd teach me some English."

"Oh, so that's what it is! If English is the problem, though, you'd do better to take lessons from your brother."

"Oh no, not from that brute! As soon as I begin to think I'm catching on, he gets angry!"

Fujiki looked up. "Chieko's such an idiot, you know," he said. "Who needs help with the English they teach in a girl's school?"

"All right, so I'm an idiot, but I'm not asking *you*. Will you, Mr. Shiomi, will you?"

I smiled wryly, glanced over the English reader open on the desk, and began reading and translating it. The girl peered at it from beside me, bending her head over the book and now and again impatiently brushing away the hair that fell over her eyes. It struck me for absolutely no reason that her pale face, seen that way in profile, wasn't as handsome as her brother's. Despite being brother and sister, the two of them had very different faces. With his cold, regular features, Fujiki probably more resembled his late father, whereas Chie's sunny looks no doubt came from her mother.

"It's warmed up, hasn't it." Fujiki's mother emerged from the kitchen carrying a tray of cups for black tea. She looked so much like her daughter that I couldn't repress a smile. I felt extremely happy.

"Finish up now, Chie-chan," she continued. "You shouldn't be bothering Mr. Shiomi this way."

The girl pouted at her. "All right, we'll have to stop there," she said resignedly and began tidying up.

"Here will do," her mother said, setting the cups out on the desk. "Come, Shinobu, come over and join us."

Fujiki came over to the desk and sat down in silence. I asked him what he'd been reading, but I'd never heard of the book he named. For a while we all discussed Chie-chan's exam.

"By the way," I asked Fujiki, "have you decided to come to the archery camp?" My heart beat fast.

"Yes, I'm going," he replied with a glance at his mother.

"Go, by all means," she said. "It's fine, as far as I'm concerned. You'll probably be going too, won't you, Mr. Shiomi?"

"Yes, of course. There's just this idea, the one I mentioned before, of hiking there over the mountains."

On the tatami I spread the General Staff Office map I'd brought. It shone white in the glare of the lamp. I pointed out the places—here's Numazu, here's Shuzenji—and they followed intently.

"There are two ways to get to Heda," I explained. "This is where the boat goes. This route, though—the road from Shuzenji over Daruma Pass—is the one I have in mind."

"I see," said Fujiki.

I'd assumed he'd agree immediately if he meant to do so at all. He wasn't one to change his mind once he'd made a decision, and he'd already had plenty of time to think about it. Now, though, he only sat there with downcast eyes, correct and expressionless.

"I recommend going over the mountains especially because I hear you're not much of a sailor," I added encouragingly. "That's true, isn't it?"

"Oh yes, he's terrible," his sister announced loudly from beside me. "On his middle-school trip to Ōshima he was sick all the way."

"Now, now, Chie-chan, you shouldn't talk about your brother that way."

"But it's *true*!"

"You weren't there yourself."

"No, but it's true anyway!" The girl suddenly exploded with mirth. "You know what happened, Mr. Shiomi? When the boat docked they apparently had to put my brother to bed for two hours in an inn at Motomura!"

"That was just bad luck. There'd been a storm, and the boat was tossing about like mad."

"And then, Mr. Shiomi, you know what? Once he was back to normal, they set off over the sand dunes to Miharayama on camels, and apparently he was sick all over again."

The girl laughed delightedly, followed by her mother, and even Fujiki couldn't help joining in. Embarrassed, I laughed a little, too. What a difference there was between this Fujiki and the cool, dispassionate one that only I knew! Why, in reacting to me, did he never show anything but that stern mask?

"How about it, then?" I asked.

Fujiki silently toyed with his teaspoon. Then, still looking down, he asked how everyone else was going to go.

"As I told you before, they're taking the boat from Numazu. It doesn't matter, though—you can walk and still get there in the afternoon."

"So are *you* walking, Shiomi?"

"Not by myself, no. Even I don't feel like doing that."

"I . . ." He fell silent again.

I knew what he was going to say. I gazed at him intently.

"I guess I'll go with everyone else," he said.

"By boat."

"Yes."

Silence fell. Fujiki put the spoon back on the saucer, propped himself up with a hand on the tatami, and stared at the map. The map looked from where I sat like the wing of an impossibly large moth.

Why? I kept asking myself. Does he really want just to do what everyone else is doing, or is it that he doesn't like me? A memory of blank despair flitted through my mind. I'd known Fujiki for no more than a year. At first he'd sought me out on every occasion. But when autumn came, and I began visiting him sometimes at his house and chatting with his mother and sister, he gradually withdrew from me. He avoided meeting or talking with me. Why did he do that? Why had he turned so cold?

"Well, I'll be going." I said it, and that was that. Chie stared at me in wide-eyed surprise. Fujiki silently folded the map. I stood up.

"I'll walk you to the station," Fujiki's mother said. "I have some shopping to do. I'll go out the back."

Fujiki, looking as melancholy as ever, accompanied me to the dimly lit *genkan* entrance. Chie clung to his shoulders, almost riding them. She poked her head out from behind him only to say good-bye.

Fujiki's mother and I walked together along the dark road. She told me all about the school excursion. Fujiki had never slept away from home before, and she'd been too anxious to sleep that night. A vague sadness overcame me while I listened. Having lost my mother as a child, I was ready to lean on her as though she were my own. *She*, I felt, would understand. So far, however, I'd never once spoken to her that way. Then through the darkness came again the scent of daphne. I remembered how happy it had made me just a while ago, on my way to the house. Ah, daphne! I murmured to myself—just that.

We parted at the platform wicket of the brilliantly lit station. "Shinobu is terribly selfish," she said politely. "I do hope you'll forgive him." I smiled uncomfortably.

After leaving her I felt very alone. The train came right away. It was empty, and the open windows let in a still chilly wind. I stared out through the darkness as the lights of the town flashed by like shooting stars. The way he'd snubbed made me sick at heart. I'd been so looking forward to the archery club camp at Heda, and now my hopes were dashed. There was no point even in going, now that I knew Fujiki disliked me. Damn, why *should* I go? Why *should* I? I closed my eyes and repeated the thought endlessly to myself, in time with the swaying of the train.

The gong rang for lunch.

Absorbed in *go*, carom, reading, chatting, and so on after the morning archery session, we all now got up together and rushed to the dining hall. Twenty arrows in a morning made for strenuous exercise, and the air was rich in salty ozone. At our age of rapid growth, nothing could stand in the way of our appetite.

In the dining hall, club members and senior advisers all claimed their seats in no particular order at the long, narrow tables. There was never any feast to fight over, anyway. Every breakfast consisted of *wakame* seaweed and miso soup, lunch of deep-fried tofu with *hijiki* seaweed simmered in soy broth, and dinner mostly of fish boiled in soy and sugar. Now and again we got sliced yellowtail sashimi, served with a mound of inedible seaweed. After the grumbling we opened cans of our own and gobbled up extra rice. The biggest talkers got the most.

In a corner of the dining hall there was a ping-pong table, and those who finished eating first gathered around it. The click of carom balls in the recreation room across the way, and the dance music blaring from a cheap record player, sounded strangely *nostalgique* once we were all gone from the dining hall.

I walked down the hallway and out toward the beach on the harbor side. It sloped down, white, and in the midday sun the sparse pines cast short shadows at my feet. The sea shone like a mirror. I strolled down the beach, studded with small shells, to the edge of the water.

There were two small, old-style boats out there on the harbor, just this side of the wharf. One of them seemed to be following the current out toward the open sea, but the other was just going around in circles. Aboard it I could see Mori, perilously bent over, working the stern oar. The fellow sculling the one a little further away was Kinoshita, whose merciless teasing of Mori, echoed by laughter closer in, carried across the water. Someone was reclining in the bow, laughing too, but I didn't recognize the voice. I watched the scene for a while and then set out along the beach. A little further on I came to a large fishing boat, hauled up on the sand. I gripped the gunwale, lifted the skirts of my *hakama*, and jumped in. The boat smelled of damp wood and, slightly, of fish. I sat down on the stern thwart, took a paperback from the fold of my robe, and began aimlessly turning the pages.

I felt sleepy. The sun was warm and the air perfectly still. I lay down uncomfortably on my back and gazed up at the small white clouds floating like cotton wool in the sky. Soon I laid the open book over my eyes and half dozed off. Tinny dance music from the record player mingled with laughing voices from across the water, making my immediate surroundings quieter still. I was at peace, I was happy, and trouble seemed very far away.

"Fujiki . . ."

The name reached me in Kinoshita's voice, and suddenly I was all ears.

"Somehow or other, the guy just seems always the same."

This was Mori's impudent, drawling voice. The sound of the oar was coming closer—Kinoshita and Mori must be returning together. I realized that at some point one of them had moved into the other's boat.

"He seems so down in the dumps, doesn't he?" The voice was Kinoshita's.

"Oh, he's probably pondering some impossible math problem. Maybe he's planning to wow the teacher again."

"The teacher?"

"Yeah, a while ago in the classroom Fujiki asked him a real poser, and the teacher had nothing more to say for a whole hour. Fujiki was embarrassed and told him it was okay, he didn't have to answer, but the teacher was really upset. I didn't even understand what the question was about."

"Well, Mori's thing is more . . ."

Mori's shrill laughter drowned him out. The sound of the oar kept coming closer.

"If that's what's eating him, no problem, but . . ."

"Why? Is there something else?"

"I dunno, but Shiomi's so out of it these days, I was wondering whether there's something going on between them."

"Those two . . ."

The voice dropped, and I couldn't catch the words. My cheeks were burning. I thought perhaps I should get up and let them know I was there.

"Yeah, Yanai's really worried about that, you know. If Fujiki's the reason Shiomi is like this, he says, he'll have Fujiki quit the club. This is just between us, though, right?"

"I wouldn't expect Yanai to understand the finer points of human feelings."

"Well, he *is* the club captain."

"He should just let it go."

"I've always thought Fujiki keeps his eyes to the ground because of Shiomi. But maybe not."

"Here we are!"

I heard the boat crunch up onto the sand. They put the oar away and talked on as they crossed the beach.

"The archery camp here is okay, but there aren't enough girls around."

"What do you expect? It's a dormitory!"

"If *that's* what it is, they should come right out and say so. I mean, look at the place! You can go all the way to the village without finding a single girl worth a second glance."

"Of course not. Actually, there's something girlish about Fujiki, isn't there? Or maybe I've been surrounded by boys for too long."

"He's only a kid, you know. He might as well still be nursing. It's strange, though. How did his mind get so far ahead of the rest of him?"

"How about you, Mori? Are you just putting it on?"

Their laughter faded away across the sand.

For a while I didn't move. The sun was getting hotter, and the fishy smell was growing. I took the book off my eyes and peered over the edge of the boat. The two of them were nowhere to be seen, and the boat heading out toward the ocean had vanished, too. Beyond the village, mist shrouded Mount Daruma.

I clambered out of the fishing boat and crossed the beach back to the lodge.

During the afternoon session I kept looking forward to getting together with Fujiki and having a talk. I hadn't spoken to him once since we arrived. This desire became irrepressible when the session was over and we'd changed back into ordinary clothes. Nonetheless, I managed to play *go* twice with Tachibana in the recreation room without letting on. He beat me soundly. Fujiki wasn't among the nearby group playing carom.

I went down the hall to Fujiki and Yashiro's room. I felt affronted as I opened the door, but I screwed up my courage and opened it anyway. Suitcases and bedding were scattered everywhere, but there was no one around. On the off chance I looked into the next room, too, but Fujiki's wasn't among the heads that turned toward me. Yashiro wasn't there either. Perhaps the two had gone off for a walk. I'd never be able to talk to Fujiki alone, though, if they were together. I slipped on some geta and stepped out into the quadrangle.

They couldn't have gone far—it wasn't long till dinner. There were four possible routes for a casual walk. The first took you toward the village, to a little park from which you could look straight across the bay at Mount Daruma. The second went through the pines behind the bathhouse and led to a tangerine orchard on a hillside facing the ocean. The third followed the beach along the bay. Lots of us went that way because you could practice sculling an old-style boat there, or do some sumo wrestling. The fourth led to the tip of the promontory. You had to walk there along the top of the breakwater or make your way through a lot of weeds. Either way it was a lonely walk, and few of us took it.

I was thinking all this over under a cherry tree when three first-year students came strolling along, singing our school dormitory song. Their leader was someone named Kimura, who'd finally managed to get himself admitted after several years of failing and was now quite full of himself. He was bawling out the song in the most sentimentally exaggerated manner, whacking at the cherry branches with his stick as he did so. The other two followed behind like mules, with smug expressions on their faces.

"How about joining us?" Kimura said.

Without a second thought I walked off. I went straight along the deserted curve of the bay as far as the breakwater, then clambered up it, geta and all. I'm not a hearty fellow like you three! I said to myself. I didn't even want that kind of heartiness.

The sea gleamed dully in the slanting light of the setting sun. Clouds hung over the horizon, drifting mass by mass toward the east. From the top of the breakwater the view of the open ocean, unlike that of the bay, suggested loneliness and desolation. From where I stood the rock dike dropped steeply away, in a jumble of boulders, to slant at last more gently down into the waves that forever washed them with their spray. There on the breakwater the sea wind was cold against my cheeks. I headed toward the tip of the dike, my heart heavy with regret. No one would ever come out here for a casual stroll. I couldn't think why I should have had to get away from those guys and their dumb self-satisfaction.

Walking over the rocks in geta was practically impossible, and I kept stopping to rest my feet. Meanwhile the sinking sun was slowly reddening layers of wispy clouds that seemed to have been brushed across the sky. I walked on for a while, watching every step, until I was too exhausted to go on and scrambled back down off the dike, on the bay side. Down there, now in shadow, thick shrubs and weeds grew between the spindly young pines. I was forcing my way through them when I raised my eyes for a moment to see, facing away from me on a rock near the end of the breakwater, the seated figure of Fujiki.

I gasped with surprise. His back, seen against those wispy, reddened clouds, conveyed a sort of forlorn dejection. I cupped my hands and hoarsely called out to him. He didn't turn around.

Perhaps I was mistaken. Hastily I forged ahead through the underbrush. The ground was uneven and my field of view closed. I was aware of nothing but my own impatience. At last, with great difficulty, I got through the brush and found myself near the point itself, amid a rubble of boulders. The breakwater had dropped low enough to merge with the rocks that covered the shore. Fujiki was nowhere to be seen.

I looked around desperately. Before me was the sea, its darkened waves sweeping with surprising speed into the bay. The tide must be high. Waves crashed gloomily on the rocks, throwing up white spray. Heavy seas were breaking, too, against the reddish cliffs across the bay entrance. Every rock glowed mottled red in the rays of the setting sun. Once you got used to the noise of the waves the place was eerily quiet.

Then I heard the dull chug-chug of the launch approaching from the bay. Blasts of its whistle echoed and re-echoed. The last launch to Numazu, I told myself. As it passed through the narrow entrance I saw the gray deck, the black stack, and the passengers scattered about on the deck. Once out on the open sea it turned right, pitching and rolling, and vanished into the distance. I looked around me again, but there was only the desolate smell of the rocky shore and the eerie silence. I started back along the edge of the bay, assuring myself over and over again that my preoccupation with Fujiki must have made me hallucinate a vision of him. On this side there was a narrow path through the pines.

It must be dinnertime by now. When I reached the lodge entrance I stopped to think a moment, then decided first to go up to my room. As I started down the dim corridor, I heard a merry voice from a room I'd assumed would be deserted. It sounded like that joker Mori. Curious, I opened the sliding door. A moldy smell assailed me. Just two of the outer shutter panels were open, admitting a dim twilight glow. I saw shadows moving. Ishii lay face up on the bed, while Mori straddled him, laughing. Lanky Ishii was waving his legs in the air, the trousers covering his skinny shanks flapping about like bats.

"What's going on? You're not fighting, are you?"

Even Ishii couldn't contain his laughter.

"This is called the *normallage*," Mori announced with shameless self-satisfaction. "Shiomi, do you know how many kinds of *normallage* there are?"

"All right, that's enough! Just get off me a minute!" said Ishii from underneath.

Mori did so, and Ishii sat up with obvious relief. He turned out to have a book with a black cover in his hand. He showed it to me.

"You see, we . . ." He snickered again. "Just to keep the record straight, Mori's the ringleader here. I'm just his assistant."

"Have a look at the book," Mori interrupted. "You'll get the idea. Of course, Shiomi, you probably don't know anything about these things."

I blushed scarlet as I leafed with affected indifference through the book. Here and there among the closely printed German sentences I noted strange illustrations.

"We're always having to look up the words in the dictionary, so we decided just to try it out in practice—it's a lot of work!"

"Ishii's not much of a partner to do it with, though," Mori remarked.

I blushed again and hastily returned the book. "Isn't it time to eat?" I murmured vaguely as I left the room. Behind me, the pair of them were still laughing.

Up in my room on the second floor, I found Tachibana propped all alone against the window frame, reading a book by the last rays of the sun. I went up to him and spat out the window.

"Where were you?" he asked.

"Umm . . . What about dinner?"

"I've eaten. You'd better get there fast."

I mumbled something and flopped down on the tatami, arms stretched wide. "I've had it," I said. The picture I'd just seen, of a man and a woman in close embrace, floated into my mind. I'd so longed to find Fujiki, but I felt as though I'd been swept off instead into some other, degenerate world.

Tachibana stood there looking down at me, mystified.

I couldn't sleep that night. Even after we turned out the light, the moon shone dimly onto the tatami through the glass door. The air was unpleasantly warm, and the scent of cherry blossoms pervaded even the room. Tachibana fell asleep right away, but I'd just had a long discussion with Kinoshita, and my eyes wouldn't close. Yanai and Hattori had gone off to the village to drink with the seniors, who were due to leave the next day. They weren't back yet.

It must have been past eleven when a raucous chorus of voices came from the recreation room, singing the popular student song "Dekansho." The sound of breaking glass disturbed the tepid air.

"Damn, they're impossible!" Kinoshita clacked his tongue in annoyance. "It's that Yanai again."

Kinoshita got up, turned on the light, quickly put his pants on, and left the room. I laid out Yanai and Hattori's bedding, then went to the window and peered through the glass. Hazy moonlight illumined the silent building next door. There was no one to be seen.

Footsteps clattered on the stairs, and in stumbled Yanai, supported on either side by Kinoshita and Hattori. They let him go, and he collapsed into a sitting position on his futon. After them came a college student, red-faced from drinking and grinning with embarrassment. "Sorry, really sorry," he said and quickly withdrew.

"What's he sorry about?" said Yanai, running his hand over his mouth.

Hattori hurriedly changed into his sleeping robe. "We're in for it," he grumbled.

"You drank too much, right?" I asked.

"Yanai can't hold his liquor, but he goes on drinking anyway."

"Wanna drink!" Yanai bawled. "Gimme another drink!"

"All right, all right, go to sleep." Kinoshita began undressing him, but Yanai went limp to stop him.

"Shiomi!" Yanai suddenly called. "Got sumthin' to say to ya."

He glared at me with his grotesquely bloodshot eyes. I see, I said to myself, so that's why you got yourself drunk! Normally Yanai was a hopeless coward.

"What is it?" I inquired.

"I, I . . ." he stammered and heaved a big sigh. Then he pulled himself together a little and began talking in great agitation. "I just don't understand you, Shiomi," he said. "We're going into our third year now, and we have a big responsibility. However," he went on, "however, there are only seven of us. Miyazawa and Nakagawa will be coming the day after tomorrow, right? Then there's you, Kinoshita, Hattori, and Tachibana, who's asleep over there—the nerve! That makes in all . . ."

He made a face and counted on his fingers.

"What kind of nut would forget *himself*?" Hattori laughed.

"That's right! Yanai Shigeo, all unworthy, has been chosen as captain, and he means to discharge his responsibility!"

"That's enough, go to bed!" Kinoshita urged him again. "And we have the archery sessions tomorrow, too."

"Shut up, scorekeeper! The thing is, there are just seven of us, and for a ten-man session we're three short. That's the way it is. There's hardly ever been a year with so few, but there's no use griping about that now. However hard we train the guys going into second year, we'd better get *our* act together or we'll lose the tournament this summer. Is that what you want?"

"Stop bitching," said Kinoshita. "Yashiro and Ishii are an asset for us, and even Fujiki and Kimura are coming along well."

"What *I* think, though, what *I* think, is that we seven are the ones who really matter. Each of us has to draw the bow right and be a model for the second-years. But you, Shiomi—what the hell do you think you're doing? You're just not putting your heart into it."

"I'm in a slump right now," I said.

"All right, so you're in a slump—so what? You're just telling me to get off your back."

Hattori laughed. "He's got something there," he said.

"That's not what I meant," I protested.

"This isn't easy to say, Shiomi, even for me," he went on, "but I just can't stand the way you're moping around over Fujiki."

"You don't understand."

"Oh, I understand! I understand, all right! We all do, right? We all know well enough you've got troubles. What I'm saying is that these troubles of yours are a waste of time."

I felt the blood drain from my face.

"That was uncalled for," I retorted. "Whatever problems I have are my own."

Yanai raised his bloodshot eyes to my face.

"Don't you give me that! We went into archery together, we studied together, we went together to plead for favorable consideration, we share joint responsibility for winning or losing a tournament. If after all that you're going to spend your time eating your heart out, do you expect us to feel good about it? To hell with Fujiki! For us, Shiomi, the one who matters is *you*!"

I remembered what Kinoshita had been saying to Mori on that boat. Surely they weren't going to have Fujiki resign from the club. I waited, ready to put up a fight if Yanai suggest anything of the kind. But he said nothing more.

"I'm with Yanai," Kinoshita put in. "To me, all this misery of yours over Fujiki is nonsense. It has nothing to do with friendship."

"Oh, but it does," I insisted loudly.

"Friendship goes two ways, though. If Yanai begins failing in school, *you* worry about him; and Yanai worries about *you* over this business of Fujiki. *That's* friendship, isn't it? This other thing—it's just you on your own, plunging ahead blind."

"It's *not!*" I shouted passionately. "In real friendship, your friend's spirit is sleeping within him like a spring at the bottom of a deep ravine, and you find that spring and drink from it. It has nothing to do with what people usually call 'bonding'—it's more mystical, it involves spiritual sympathy. That's what I'm looking for in Fujiki. To me, *that's* real friendship."

"I see," said Hattori in a mocking tone. "Such is the fruit of Shiomi Shigeshi's platonic meditations. Fujiki's a pretty lad, it's true—he's just what the Greeks must have meant by *ephebos*. But all this talk about 'spirit' goes too far."

"That's why I keep telling you all that you just don't understand."

"I agree, 'spirit' doesn't really come into it," Kinoshita said calmly. "It's the element of the *physique* that you're in love with."

"No, it's not!" I shouted. "You've got it all wrong!"

But I could see no way to explain how I felt. Yanai, his drunkenness apparently past, flopped back on his bed. You could hear the distant waves.

"It's late. Let's get to sleep." This was the voice of Tachibana, not sleeping after all, heard unexpectedly from where he lay nearby. "Come on, Yanai, you get some sleep, too. You'll end up with a cold."

Yanai started taking off his jacket, so Kinoshita snuggled down into his bedding. Tachibana got up and switched off the light.

"Shiomi's well aware of all this, you know," he said as he stood there. "You really shouldn't go rubbing salt into people's wounds like that."

In the faintly moonlit darkness I lay there wide-eyed, staring up at the ceiling. A dim glow filled the room, and the blossoms' sweetness had something comforting about it. You just don't understand, I said over and over to myself, listening to the waves.

What *is* the element of the *physique*? I kept wondering helplessly about this, leaning against the breakwater.

Every cherry tree in sight was in magnificent bloom. Layer on layer of blossoms drank in the warm sunlight, and each bowstring twang seemed to start a little shower of petals. A while ago I'd stood on the sidelines to watch Fujiki shoot his arrows, and it had been beautiful, the way the petals settled on his single white, bared shoulder. But a suffocating sort of sensation had then come over me, and I'd fled before the end of the session.

Village children used to come and play there almost every day. They'd roll hoops in their straight-sleeved kimono, dark blue with white splashes. Fujiki and Mori got to be good friends with them, and they'd roll hoops with them. The steel rod with a curved end—something like a steel chopstick—hitting the steel hoop as it bounded along made a pleasant ringing sound. Even where I was now, the ringing and jingling from beyond the pinewood struck the ear as pleasantly cool.

No doubt Fujiki was tripping lightly along, his kimono sleeves tied up out of the way. Pale cheeks flushed, steel rod in his delicate hand, peering ahead round-eyed, he'd be racing nimbly up and down the bumps and dips in the uneven ground . . . Didn't this fantasy then have something to do with the *physique*? The bashfulness that kept me even from entering the bath with him—wasn't this, too, perhaps the *physique*?

"What are you thinking about, Shiomi?"

There beside me stood that devil Yashiro, his faced creased with a knowing grin.

"Shiomi, I have something to tell you. It's a secret, though."

Why did I feel somehow humiliated whenever he turned up? Ah, that smile! However I might dislike him, with his sly smile he always seemed to see straight through me.

"Fujiki, you see . . ." He paused as though for dramatic effect, eyes on my profile.

"Fujiki may be about to quit the club."

"Who told you that?"

"Fujiki himself, of course. I can't be sure he really will, though."

Without another word he strolled off, whistling, toward the archery range. That's impossible! I insisted to myself. I could still hear the jingling of the hoops, mingled with laughing voices. Fujiki quit the club? Why, he'd never do a dumb thing like that. Still, I'd never once spoken to him since we got here. Surely Yanai wouldn't have put pressure on him?

With a stifling feeling I climbed to the top of the breakwater. The open ocean's boundless blue filled my gaze. Standing there looking out over the waves, I just wanted to go somewhere else alone, far, far away.

Our three college-student seniors had decided to hike back over Daruma Pass on the day of the village festival. So many village people came wandering out toward the point on that day that each year we'd just give up our archery sessions and go out for a good time. It was Kinoshita who suggested that this year we should leave the younger students in charge and see our seniors off as far as the pass. The five of us set off that morning with them. Miyazawa and Nakagawa, who were joining the archery camp late, were supposed to arrive over the pass that day.

Our group stayed together all the way along the stone-paved path, beside a sea still covered here and there by dwindling wisps of morning mist, but once we'd passed the village center, already livening up for the festival, and turned right at the sweet shop Akizuki, we gradually strung ourselves out over some distance. We made our way through terraced fields while larks sang high in the clear, bright sky, and the monotonous beating of festival drums reached us from below. The path became steep, and you could see when you looked back a wider and wider expanse of ocean.

I was walking with the college student Kasuga. Puffing away at a cigarette, he bent over now and again neatly to pick, say, a violet. With a conjuror's delicacy he'd remove the petals and give me a little botany lecture. The mountains were silent, the sky so flawless as to be almost blank. Nonetheless, intimations of futility, like mist on a mirror, cast a faint shadow over my consciousness.

Fujiki was now with Yashiro, Mori, Ishii, and the others. What were they doing? Sharp pangs of jealously toward Yashiro, who could talk and laugh with Fujiki any time he liked, kept tormenting me. I could only slink around out of sight, never exchanging more than a few words with Fujiki. If on top of that he quit the club, then the tie between us would be broken forever. We were in different years, studying different subjects, and we'd never see each other even in the dormitory or in the classroom. That might be for the best, though. What was the point of nursing this useless attachment day after day?

I made up my mind. "I'm thinking of quitting the club," I announced to Kasuga.

"Quitting the club?" he answered slowly, still gazing at the violet's calyx in his hand.

"Right."

"Where'd you suddenly get *that* idea from? What's the matter? Things aren't going too well with Yanai? Did you quarrel?"

"No, no, nothing like that."

"Yanai means well, you know." Kasuga dropped the flower and gave me an encouraging glance.

"My archery's in a terrible slump," I explained earnestly, "and, really, I'm not that interested in sports anyway. So if it seems I'm out of place in the club and just making trouble for the others . . ."

"You're exaggerating. There isn't any trouble."

"But I feel unwelcome. I can't do anything about feeling so isolated, but I don't want to make trouble for other people as well."

"I don't think I get what you're talking about."

Kasuga drew a cigarette pack from his pocket, took one himself, and held the pack out toward me. I'd only just learned how to smoke at the school commemoration day festival in February, and I hadn't yet picked up the habit, but with a polite little bow I took one. Kasuga struck a match and lit it for me. The smoke drifted languidly away as we began walking again.

"You're a loner, I know," Kasuga said. "It makes a difference. I see no contradiction, though, between being solitary and being a member of a sports club. Solitude isn't the real thing if it can't survive a club's communal life, with its shared goals and training. You'll never get anywhere with this feeble solitude of yours, as though you'd yourself shut into an eggshell."

"I agree. But what if it hurts people?"

"You think that? That it's of a kind to hurt others?"

"No, I mean that the one getting hurt is me."

"How?"

"Er . . . by love, I suppose."

"By love? I'd say real solitude goes beyond any possibility of hurt and makes the most painful love bearable. To me it's something positive and spiritually strong. For example, it's the condition of someone absorbed in prayer. Before God, prayer is human weakness itself, but at the human level it has an inviolable strength. Solitude strikes me as being much the same."

"Is it really that strong, though? Me, I just get myself hurt all the time."

"Well, someone's bound to get hurt when the love between two people is unequal and out of balance."

"I suppose you're right," I said.

"In that case, though, the power of love and the power of solitude are out of proportion to each other. The one of the two whose love is greater usually ends up being hurt by the other, whose love isn't yet great enough. Even then, though, the right thing to do is to uphold that greater love. Being loved is like bathing in sun-warmed water—there's nothing lonely about it. To love greatly is to risk one's own solitude. Isn't that the real way to live, despite the risk of hurt? I'd call it perhaps the way to nurture solitude and refine it."

I felt as though Kasuga was talking particularly about me. He fell silent for a while, then went on with a gentle smile, "I have the impression that Fujiki, that first-year student, is the cause of all your troubles, right?"

I could tell my cheeks were burning. Embarrassed, I tossed my cigarette away.

"Everyone goes through this, you know, sooner or later, although you're too involved in the experience now to understand that. I'd say it's not unlike a bout of measles. In childhood, you see, we're *asexuel*, and then when we grow up a bit we become *bisexuel*—we're attracted to both girls and boys. Then there's a period when we're *homosexuel*. After that we become adults. So right now you're in a transitional phase that you're bound to get over, like measles."

"This isn't just a phase," I protested. "This is real love, I know it is, love like no other ever again. That's why I'm feeling terrible. To call it 'transitional' . . ."

"Right, sorry if I overstated it a bit. Anyway, I take it there's nothing to feel guilty about in your feelings for Fujiki?"

Something to feel guilty about, some element of the *physique* . . . A discordant note rang deep within me, and I felt a touch of rebellion.

"No, nothing whatever to feel guilty about."

"I see." He nodded. "So you're calling it friendship?"

"That's right. To me, it's true friendship."

"Fine. To my mind, though, in a *homosexuel* relationship the two people concerned seek solitude as a couple and build a secret wall around their shared solitude. The presence or absence of this wall determines whether or not the relationship is *abnormal*. They inevitably feel guilty about themselves and so prefer to cut themselves off. They never try, you see, to go beyond their wall into normal society. But friendship has no wall. As brotherly love or love of one's neighbor it can spread far and wide."

"Exactly! That's just what *I* think. There's this beautiful soul and that soul's way of seeing the world. Of course, the person in question never imagines that his soul is beautiful. That modesty is exactly what I love in Fujiki. I alone understand his soul. Discovering this beauty, this purity in a human soul has made my own impure soul beautiful, too, and it's allowed me to see others with beautiful eyes. That's how I see it. A spiritual refining process: that's what I like to call it. For me the process began with my discovery of this soul, and I believe it can help every one of us to live more beautifully and more happily."

Waves of rapture swept through me as we talked. No one else understands these things—this longing for the enchantment of an unblemished soul, this intoxication of love, this insight illuminating every corner of consciousness, this soaring feeling of being drawn upward toward the angels . . .

"So what about Fujiki?" Kasuga calmly inquired.

His question, though not ill-meant, broke the spell. The tide of exaltation quickly receded, leaving behind it only regrets like seaweed streaming from the rocks to which it still clung, and a flabby, jellyfish-like feeling of powerlessness. I stumbled as though suddenly blindfolded along a mountain trail bright in the noonday sun.

"Fujiki doesn't know," I replied.

Kasuga lit another cigarette. We'd climbed fairly high by now.

"Why does loving someone mean hurting him?" I asked.

"I'd say you're the one who's getting hurt," Kasuga answered. "For Fujiki being hurt or not isn't even an issue, as long as all that's happening is that somebody loves him. You, though, Shiomi—you can't go on doing this to yourself. If you really grow up and achieve the strength of solitude, then you'll no longer hurt yourself or anyone else. Love that hurts only you is for boys."

"Hasn't this ever happened to you, Kasuga?"

"Me? Yes, I've been hurt, too. Can't you tell?"

A shadow passed over his face, but he quickly recovered his mood. "Maybe this is off the subject," he said, "but at any rate, you really must give up your idea of quitting the club. You took up archery two years ago now, and we've been together ever since, so I'm responsible for you. If you can't live where life has put you, you can't live anywhere."

We walked on in silence. The cryptomeria plantations came to an end, and we found the others, who'd gone on ahead, sitting there waiting for us near the top of the pass, enjoying a sweeping view. Once reunited we opened our lunch boxes and chatted together. The breeze across the tender grass of the summit felt good on our sweaty cheeks. Heda Bay looked like a blue pool, and the sea beyond it resembled a glittering, silvery river. The village and cape surrounding the bay were all one cloud of cherry blossoms, and when you looked up, there was Fuji, floating above the spring mists. The whole view might just as well have been a postcard, and we complained to each other how trite it was. Just before the oldest ones left, the long-awaited Miyazawa and Nakagawa turned up, further heightening the emotion of the moment. We took farewell photographs and waved on and on as they started down the trail. At last the receding figure of Kasuga, following the others at a leisurely pace, vanished around a bend.

It was still early to go all the way back down, so we decided to stop off along the river at Daigyōji temple. Cherry trees in bloom lined the bank, and we found the grounds similarly overflowing with blossoms when we crossed the bridge and went in through the gate. We rinsed our faces in the cold water from the well and climbed the ladder to the bell tower, where we sat on the railing. The ancient cherry tree near the well had only two branches, both on the same side, covered eccentrically with blood-red flowers.

With two new faces among us we talked away more volubly than ever. Miyazawa stirred our envy with his account of a new movie he'd just seen, Hattori teased him, Kinoshita displayed his superior knowledge, and Yanai declared that movies were a bore. Everyone said his piece and drew me now and again into the conversation. Their kindness aroused in me a feeling of intense gratitude. I thought back to those who had come here last year and who since then had left the club. Among the seven of us I was now the youngest, and what had happened two evenings ago could hardly fail to bring home to me that even I had my place in the group. No, I couldn't just quit the archery club. I'd have to stay with them, suffer alone, and try to keep my troubles to myself. Having sworn not to join the Heda camp, I'd now put more than of half its calendar behind me, and the height of the cherry blossom season was beginning to pass. I hadn't managed a single conversation with Fujiki; instead I'd surrounded myself, of my own free will, with a wall of dreams and isolation. What I needed most to do was to put action before thought, speech before silence, and declarations of love before mere waiting. The thing was to have Fujiki understand me and to have him, through love, grow to love. He was still a child, perhaps, but what was the point of my suffering all alone, from a distance, without a clue as to what he was thinking or why he wouldn't speak? It was a human being I loved, not an idol; a reality, not a dream; the present, not some remote future. If my love for Fujiki was misguided, then I would just have to impose on myself an even stricter solitude. That course was certainly preferable to deceiving myself and waiting for something that would never happen.

We made our way back to the point, singing our dormitory song, through all the commotion of the village's spring festival. Vigorous young men in white headbands shouldered their shrine's sacred palanquin. Now and again we stopped to gawk at them, and the beat of the great festival drum followed us all the way back.

That evening I got together with Fujiki, and we talked.

When your resolve keeps shifting and wavering, the weight of it all burdens your consciousness until, ever so slowly, you finally make your decision; but then it can happen that the whole problem just slips your mind. As far as I could see, I'd failed so far to get together with Fujiki only because I hadn't mustered the courage to do so. I could meet him at any time if I actually wanted to—here we both were, after all, in the same college lodge, on this same narrow cape. So, no more vacillation, no more cowardice! But once I'd got that far, I could easily have forgotten the whole thing and spent the evening drinking in the recreation room.

On the way back from Daigyōji, Yanai had filled an empty beer bottle with sake, the idea being for us to drink it secretly right there in the recreation room, in the way of a welcome party for Miyazawa and Nakagawa. You couldn't just drink openly in front of the first-year students while the camp was in progress, and there wouldn't be enough to go around if any seniors happened to barge in. So the second-years sat by themselves in a circle, under a bare light bulb, to pass the sake around in a teacup.

"Hey, we'll never get drunk *this* way!" Hattori exclaimed, laughing. "This might as well be a wake!"

"Ideas, anyone?" Kinoshita put in.

"We have so little," Miyazawa sighed. "How about cutting what we haven't yet drunk with water?"

"Watered sake? No thanks!" Yanai roared. "Let's just sing the dormitory song and keep the cup circulating. That way we should all get one drink, anyway. What do you say?"

"We'll be caught, won't we, if we make a lot of noise?"

"Who cares? Let's do it!"

We all stood up, joined hands, and began our chorus. The cup sped around until the song came to an end.

"This is great!" Miyazawa hooted wildly.

We went on to belt out a medley of such songs, sentimental or crude, and while catching our breath between them we each got a sip. Not being much of a drinker, I soon ended up with a headache. "Hey, you're not leaving, you know!" Hattori tried to hold me back, but I shook off his grip and went outside.

The sand was wet with dew as I crossed it toward the bay. The moon wasn't up yet, and Mount Daruma stood out in black silhouette against the sky. Fishing fires burned here and there across the water, and you could still hear the monotonous thump of the great drum. I went down to the water's edge, squatted on the sand, and gazed at the phosphorescent creatures glowing in each breaking wave. That forgotten decision of mine then came back to me, together with bitter regret. What mattered most was certainly not getting drunk and having a good time.

That was when I ran into Fujiki.

"Feeling bad, Shiomi?"

His voice brought me immediately to my feet. Not even I could tell whether my unsteadiness had to do with what I'd drunk or with the impact of surprise.

"Fujiki!" I managed to exclaim before my voice failed. Then I stared at the dark figure approaching me along the water's edge, as though to make certain who it was. Fujiki's cape collar was open. He peered into my face.

"You've been drinking, Shiomi?" he asked.

"Actually, Fujiki, there's something I've been meaning to talk to you about."

"Why would you want to drink?" There was reproach in his gentle voice.

The chorus over there in the recreation room was still going on. Moisture dripped from the branches of the pines.

"I wanted to talk to you. I'm afraid there may be a misunderstanding between us."

"A misunderstanding? I don't think so."

I shivered slightly. The breeze felt cold. "How about a walk?" I said with an inviting glance. It was too dark to make out his expression, but he started off with me without a word. How to begin, though? What was it most important to say? My head was still throbbing.

"I'm having a bad time," I said.

"Did you drink *that* much, Shiomi?"

He glanced at me, giving his voice the same endearing quality as when we'd first known each other. I shook my head.

"I just don't know what to do, you see. They're saying you're going to quit the club."

"Me?"

"Am I that much of a problem for you?"

"Wait a minute! I don't know what they're talking about. I may become a day student, but that's all."

"Really? Yanai didn't say anything to you?"

"Yanai?" He sounded astonished.

"All right. I only heard it from Yashiro, after all. I suppose he was worrying needlessly about you."

I heaved a sigh of relief. We were walking through the pines. Darkness surrounded us, while fishing lights glittered on the sea. I loved this moment with Fujiki as though it were eternity itself, and I'd have been completely happy if only it had lasted forever. I sighed again. He apparently mistook my meaning.

"Yes, he was. Everyone seems unnecessarily worried about me. I'd never do that. Shiomi, I really don't want you to suffer,"

"I can't help it, you know. I'm just like that."

"I hate the idea that it's because of *me*, though."

"That's what love does to you," I said.

Love: the word should have brought him up short. I fell silent for fear of having said too much, but he didn't say another word.

"Why are you *suffering*, though?" he finally whispered. "Aren't you just showing off your troubles for my benefit?"

"Absolutely not."

"So you drink, you scare me with all this talk of suffering, and you've got what you wanted. I object."

"No, no, you don't understand. All you see is the surface."

"Perhaps so. How am I to know, though, if not from the surface, whether you're really suffering or not? Here I am, completely worthless, and apparently you see me as something quite different. Visible objects, surfaces are all we have around us in life, you know—there's no escaping them."

"That's not true. From that visible world you can go on into the invisible. That's what love is. To love is to remake the world. If you loved . . . You see what I mean, right? Our spirits would soar beyond human experience, into the world of pure ideas. No time, no space, only endless joy . . ."

"There you go again with your Plato . . ."

"Ah, you just don't get it."

"No, I don't."

We fell silent. The breeze picked up a little, stirring the pine boughs against the starry sky, and vapor gathered over the sea. My eyes were now more used to the dark, and I could make out the pale shape of his face. This is it, my inner voice urged me passionately, you *must* speak now, you *must* make him understand.

"Why don't you get it, though, I wonder. Only love lifts us above our earthly solitude and into the realm of pure ideas, the only place where true living is possible. But you . . ."

"But I'm all right as I am," Fujiki murmured. "Everything you're saying is just words, Shiomi, just empty words."

"No, really, Fujiki, I'm serious. There's absolutely nothing impure about my feelings."

"Impure? What do you mean?"

"Er . . ." I couldn't go on.

I no longer had any idea how to explain myself to him. I sighed. And I love you so much! I murmured as though to myself.

"But I don't want your love," Fujiki replied distinctly.

"You don't? Why? I'm not good enough for you?"

"No. *I'm* not good enough for *you*."

"You can't be serious. Your spirit is so pure, so beautiful."

"I'm a worthless, commonplace human being. I know all about what I'm like. And besides . . ."

"What?"

"Besides, loving someone . . ."

He hesitated a little. I had the feeling I'd made him blush.

"Go on. What is it?"

"Loving someone means wanting that person to love *you*, doesn't it? If you love me, you must expect me to love you back, right?"

"For me, just loving is enough."

"I think you're wrong. You'd have no reason to suffer, would you, if that was true."

"My suffering . . ."

I hardly knew what to say. I'd never imagined Fujiki pressing me this hard. *Could* there really be a kind of love that asked no return of love at all? In the end surely I, too, dreamed that Fujiki would come to love me, and that the two of us, bound by love, would then know that ideal world. I had no intention of lying to him, but I was afraid he might recoil from me if I mentioned this.

The moon must have risen, because his face now stood out, pale, in the shadow of the pines.

"Shiomi," he said suddenly, "I don't want to see you suffer. Please, listen to me. However much you may suffer, I just can't love you back."

"You dislike me that much, then?" I asked hoarsely.

"No, not at all. It's just that I can't love anyone. I'm incapable of love."

"Nonsense!"

"I'm afraid of it."

He blurted out the words in such obvious distress that I unconsciously reached out to him. I grasped his hand under his cape. It was icy cold.

"That's only because you're still so young," I said.

"No, that's not it. Loving means being responsible, right? That degree of responsibility is beyond me."

"You're talking about responsibility?"

"To love means to choose, and when you've made that choice, you remain responsible for it, don't you, to the death?"

"Of course."

"That scares the daylights out of me. Besides, we're already born to love certain people—our parents, our brothers and sisters, and so on. I lost my father when I was a child, and my mother is bringing me up alone, so the more I feel my mother's love, the more heavily—it almost chokes me sometimes—I feel responsible for returning it. The only reason I study so hard is that I want to make her happy. And then there's my sister, Chieko. No, really, the burden is already too much for me. With all that I can't just go and choose someone else on my own."

"But you're making it all so much more difficult than it really is. This business of being responsible . . ."

"I just want to drop it."

Fujiki gently withdrew his hand from mine and squatted down as though exhausted. I remained standing before him, while a sort of vertigo spread to every corner of my consciousness. Poor Fujiki! Poor faint-hearted, timorous boy! You know nothing, do you! The ardor, the mystery of love, the still greater joy of responsibility—why, you have absolutely no conception of any of it!

"I don't flatter myself, you know, with the hope that you'll come to love me. I'm perfectly satisfied loving you just the way I do now."

"But I don't *want* you loving me," Fujiki said very low, squatting there beneath the pines, shaded even from the moonlight.

"Why? You have no responsibility at all."

"*You* do, though, don't you, Shiomi?"

"Yes, I do, now I've chosen you as a friend."

"But for me that's a burden. It's suffocating, the idea of you thinking of me all the time in that serious way. I just want you to leave me alone."

"You don't believe in friendship?"

"Why should I?"

"But, Fujiki, don't we make the world more beautiful for ourselves by believing in other people? How pathetic we'd all be if there was no such thing as love! Don't you agree?"

"You're just playing with ideas."

"Why do you say that? High-school and dormitory life, then—what is it, if it isn't based on friendship?"

"I don't know. I suspect it's a lot more conventional than that. Mutual respect, mutual forbearance—that's about what it amounts to."

"How insipid! Is there no room in it, then, for spiritual joy?"

"That's all *I* ask of it, at any rate. Friendship like Yashiro's and Ishii's does me fine. I don't need any special friendship. For me, this beautiful love you keep talking about is just a bother. And what can any of us do, anyway? We're all born to walk a particular path. The best we can do is keep our eyes on the ground in front of us and not get lost."

"What a depressing way to look at it! Why don't you ever look up at the stars?"

"I can't."

Fujiki stood up. The dim moonlight filtering through the pines lit his face. "How about heading back?" he said.

We went out onto the sand. The muffled thud of the big drum still reached us across the waves, but the chorus of voices singing the dormitory songs had stopped. Fujiki put up the collar of his cape and walked beside me, his head hung low. With every step this precious chance receded irretrievably into the distance. He hadn't refused to love me. No, he'd refused to accept my love. What did I have left?

"Listen, Fujiki," I began, to break the unbearable silence, "I take it then that you mean to follow your path alone, without help from anyone?"

"That's right," he whispered.

"We humans are so helpless, though! Do you really think you can do that?"

"Helpless, yes, and nobody more so than me. But what good would it do to superimpose our two solitudes? Wouldn't that be like adding zero to zero?"

"But doesn't this solitude of ours mean precisely that we need love?"

"I just want to drop the subject," he repeated weakly.

I stopped walking. A fishing boat drawn up on the sand lay in the moonlight like a beached monster. As though caught in a bad dream, I watched Fujiki continue on into the distance. I was losing him, losing him. Clinging and despair swept over me like a succession of breaking and receding waves.

"No!" I shouted, running after him. Fujiki turned his pale face toward me.

"No, I can't accept that! Look, Fujiki, I'll keep my distance. All you have to do is be what you are. Whether I suffer or not, you're not responsible. I'll do my best not to. I'll do everything I can so as not to be a burden to you. Just don't reject me for loving you. Can you do that, Fujiki?"

"But this is going nowhere, nowhere at all," he repeated sadly.

"Please! I'm begging you! This love is what I live for! Call it just an idea, call it a dream of mine, call it anything you like! Just don't condemn me for it, please! Please, won't you reconsider?"

Fujiki nodded weakly, like a flower drooping in the wind.

"Good! Tomorrow night we're all having a party at Akizuki. Let's go together, then. We can have another talk on the way. All right?"

Fujiki nodded and started walking. I stayed where I was till he disappeared, then headed down toward the sea. A rough log pier jutted out into the water. With faltering steps I made my way to the end, sat down, and vacantly watched the oncoming waves.

Phosphorescent creatures glowed silver as each wave struck the pilings. Although dim in the moonlight, the phosphorescence tossed about eerily in the darkness under the pier. That pale glow spoke to my mood. Was love futile, then, I wondered, unreal, a mere fantasy? Wouldn't it be better to choose death, rather than suffer this way?

I sat there for ages, wet with the night dew. Just as millions of primitive creatures drifted in the sea before me in a pale silver glow, so the will not to give up and the seduction of death swirled and glowed in my mind. I forced myself to believe that by tomorrow evening Fujiki would have changed his mind. There was still hope. Another inner voice, though, went on whispering like the endless succession of waves, "It's all over. This evening's talk with Fujiki failed, and no miracle can give me any hope for tomorrow evening."

Tomorrow evening: something extraordinary did happen then, nonetheless.

So far, so good with my writing. Writing a little this way every day has taken me back in time to the past I'd lost, and vividly recovered the misery I went through when I was eighteen. What a difference, though, between my suffering now and then! Back then, I was tempted any number of times to end my life, and I stood trembling at the edge of that fascinating abyss. Death kept its distance, however, and for all its appeal, at the last moment I could never manage to act. I lived blindly, instinctively, without a will of my own. Living was easy; life was sweet. In the end, no pain of love ever killed me.

Now the stench of death surrounds me. Living is effort, a duty. I harbor death within me, and before my eyes a procession of people passes into death. The patients who die in this sanatorium are all young. They've known only war, poverty, and sickness. Every one of them has had a miserable end. What kind of youth can they have ever enjoyed? What joy can they have ever tasted in life?

They—no, I should say we—live with death every day, but I can't pretend to see anything heroic in that. Every one of us humans walks the valley of the shadow of death. I knew even then, when the spring sunshine of Heda brightened my youth and the scent of cherry blossoms surrounded me, that death had his eye on us all and awaited us down the road. People just don't grasp that, though. The wings of death are always fluttering near, today as yesterday, but people go cheerfully about their lives and notice nothing. At the very instant when the war ended, when the hateful shadow of death vanished from daily life and we imagined ourselves living henceforth in peace, even then death awaited us as before. Leprosy, tuberculosis, cancer—many diseases beyond the reach of medical science sharpened their claws for us as ever, while in the name of civilization mankind greedily manufactured new weapons. What good is a civilization so cursed that, when the least life lost is indescribably precious, it still condones wholesale slaughter? What is human knowledge worth, if it serves only to devise new wars and new weapons of war?

On the battlefield I saw many comrades die begging for a drink of water. Now, in the sanatorium, I've seen many patients die without being able to afford a single dose of streptomycin. Their faces come back to me, as do those of several friends I was with at Heda who are gone from this world. Kinoshita, our treasurer, came down with tuberculosis in college and died after a brief period under care. There was no surgery then for the disease, only prolonged bed rest. Mori died in the war. Bouncy, mischievous Mori was serving on a destroyer when he went down with his ship off the Philippines. Kasuga died, too. Mobilized as an army doctor, he succumbed in the South Seas to an illness contracted at the front. He's the one who told me, on the trail up to Daruma Pass, that he, too, had been hurt, but I have no idea what that hurt consisted of. Everyone suffers, though, and goes to death in pain. Having lost contact with my friends from back then, I can only imagine that many others, too, have fallen victim to war, disease, or disaster. Each of them will have died his own death.

It's Fujiki's death, though, that troubles me most on sleepless nights. Fujiki Shinobu died of septicemia in the winter vacation of his third year in high school. He was still getting top grades and was planning to study physics in college when, during that vacation, he went to stay with an uncle in a village about an hour and a half from Tokyo. Of course he meant also to continue studying. This uncle belonged to a long line of doctors in the village and enjoyed wide respect, but his nephew came down with tonsillitis there, and septicemia followed. He died after three days of unrelieved misery. Absolutely nothing could be done for him, even though he was right there in a doctor's house. His condition wouldn't be life-threatening nowadays, since sulfonamides are available, but back then septicemia meant certain death. Now medicine advances step by step, but how many precious lives are lost in the meantime?

Fujiki Shinobu died in his nineteenth year. A helpless rage against his death still blazes up inside me. Why do some die so young? The gods, they say, envy their gifts, but perhaps it's more that the gods abduct them to protect the purity of their memory. The idea of a beautiful soul is probably just a fantasy, and by now I have trouble believing it myself. Back then, though, my love for Fujiki reflected his beauty back to me as in a mirror. There's no point in nursing vain regret. He was alone, I was alone, and the two of us were never able to love each other. Why, I wonder? This futile question is all I have left.

After the Heda archery camp, we returned to begin the new school year. Fujiki became a day student, though, while I remained in the dormitory, and little by little we grew apart. Now and again I visited him at his house, where I spent time also with his mother and his sister, Chieko. I had no more intimate talks with him. Alone I dreamed my dreams and abandoned them. He stayed away from the archery camp the following spring. I just walked the sandy beach of the point, smoking cigarettes. Then I graduated and became a linguistics student in college. Fujiki and I grew even further apart. The next winter, every possibility involving him came to an end.

I knew Fujiki for less than three years and was close to him for only the first. More than ten years have now passed since he died, but just as we affect others merely by being alive, those who are already gone continue to affect the living. A person lives on, even after returning to dust and ashes, as long as someone still clearly remembers the things he did, the things he said, his ways, his sensitivities, the thoughts that were his alone. As those who knew him pass on in their turn, the posterity in which he survives then shrinks until the last of them is gone, and he dies a second, final death. Thereafter he appears no more among the living.

However, this extended life, depending entirely on the memory of the living, is always in peril. So the living must continually renew their memory of the dead and share their life with them. They must accept as their natural duty not only to mourn the dead, but also to try to call back the life that the dead have lost. They must be like Orpheus, the musician, who followed his wife Eurydice, dead of snakebite, all the way down to the realm of death.

But what does it mean when someone dies young? What can redeem so tragic, so random a loss? After Fujiki died this question often filled me with helpless frustration and regret. If only he'd been able to leave some accomplishment behind him, it might have helped a little to lighten my grief. He was never able to achieve anything, though. You could hardly say that he had lived at all. Precisely for that reason, though, his spirit lingers on, unsullied, in my memory. He was a youth endowed with a beautiful spirit, and I feel somehow purified whenever I remember him. Whenever I return in thought to Arcadia, I feel Fujiki still living in me, like the purest music.

In the end the dead never return; and presumably I, too, will soon die. I don't believe in life after death, nor do I expect any reunion with Fujiki's spirit. For me the world will end with my death, and it will also kill the memory of Fujiki within me. With my death, Fujiki will die that second time. Until then, though, until I die, Fujiki will be with me, sounding in my soul like beautiful music. Surely a life that leaves the impression of music is priceless, however short.

The New Year decorations had just come down, and a stiff north wind was blowing. Far up in the infinite sky dancing kites broadcast the humming of their strings. Early that morning I boarded a train from Ueno. Late the evening before a telegram had informed me that Fujiki's condition was grave, but the terse message gave no details. The train made slow progress across the wintry plain, while my anxiety grew.

I can't clearly recapture the impressions left by that tumultuous day. By the time I rushed up to his uncle's place it was all over. The house was an old one, set on a spacious lot that included a scattering of other buildings. I was taken to the upper floor of a sort of little garden cottage, and a gust of incense assailed me the moment I reached the top of the stairs.

The floor of the six-mat room was covered with bedding, and a white cloth had been laid over Fujiki's face. Beyond the bedding I saw his mother, collapsed in tears. I knelt in the doorway and bowed in respectful greeting, hands to the floor.

How thoroughly death had changed everything in an instant! I hardly recognized Fujiki's mother. Her lips trembled with instinctive clinging beyond her power to release, and with grief akin to fear. I listened in a daze, uncomprehending, to her account of what had happened. After three days of unbroken agony he'd managed one cry of "Mother!" and then spat out a flood of blood. How could someone (and not just anyone, but Fujiki) die that simply? My mind was in turmoil. I wanted to die with him, and yet there I was, trying to comfort (even at such times we humans still find something to say) his utterly distraught mother. What can I have been thinking? They said his face was terribly changed, and I didn't even remove the cloth to look at him. (Was it discretion? Was I afraid? Had shock just paralyzed me? I'd never been able to say a word of farewell, and that sorrow kept gnawing at my heart.) Instead I simply stared, stunned, at the flower-patterned quilt and the ceremonial dagger placed upon it.

My impressions from that afternoon are even more confused. The body was moved to the main house, where a priest intoned the sutras. I remember nothing, though. I have no idea who was there. I felt nothing even resembling grief.

That evening the coffin containing the body was loaded onto a wagon, which men then drew off toward the crematorium outside the village. The glow of sunset filled the sky, and soaring flames seemed to lick the clouds. The wagon—actually, just a cart normally used for transporting vegetables and so on—bumped along the rocky road in a biting wind. On it rode the coffin. It was a long, slow way. The shadow of the procession fell on the rippling water of flooded paddies. Beside the wagon walked Fujiki's mother and Chieko. Both looked much smaller than usual.

The crematorium stood in a grove of trees. It looked like a charcoal kiln. I stood somewhat apart and watched the crematorium workers shift the coffin. Then I must have lost track of time. The first stars were showing when smoke emerged from the low chimney and rose into the sky. This smoke was the fragility of life itself, but my nerves were in such a state that I felt only a tingle of instinctive misgiving.

The procession started back again. The empty wagon followed the way it had come. Smoke from the cremation must have risen through the night. I turned back for a last glimpse of it against a darkening sky. Orion hung aloft, as though at any moment the wind might sweep it away. Already the stars were twinkling up from paddies covered by a thin film of ice.

It was then that a memory flashed into my mind: the strange, phosphorescent glow of those sea creatures around the pier on the cape; myself, staring at it; and Fujiki repeating, "But this is going nowhere, nowhere at all." This unexpected rush of memory pierced my heart and made my steps unsteady.

"But this is going nowhere." My love for him, although great, had indeed gone nowhere; and Fujiki, who had rejected it, was now gone from this earth. Love, solitude, clinging, rejection— none of it had gone anywhere. Loving and living had all been in vain. So it was for the boy who could never love anyone, the boy who could walk only the path laid out for him; and so it was for me, too, who had loved him so much.

Orion swam for a moment, as though dissolving in water, and fell in drops from my eyes.

It was the day of our party at Akizuki, and that morning a stiff breeze was whistling through the pines. Several times during our archery session we remarked that this meant the end of the blossoms. Restless, I managed nothing good with my bow. The blizzard of flying petals seemed to be whirling straight into my heart.

The party was to begin at seven, and till then our time was free. Little groups of particular friends hastily ate an early dinner or strolled about, not wanting to miss a moment of the spring evening. To shake off Tachibana, who seemed to want to stick with me, I picked my moment to go out into the quadrangle. Fujiki and I had never agreed on a time to meet, and I was afraid that we might miss each other after all. I leaned against the trunk of a cherry tree while mounting anxiety gripped me. Now and again I spotted someone in the entrance to the lodge, but of Fujiki there was no sign. I made up my mind to go back to the lodge and look into his room. It was empty. There was no one in the other rooms, either. In great agitation I rushed out again and ran toward the beach, which afforded a clear view. Twilight was turning to night.

On entering the pinewood I heard voices down by the water. Some way from the pier, a fishing boat stood out in the last light of day. I was making my way through the wood when with great surprise I saw Fujiki walking through the trees a short distance ahead of me, in the same direction. I called his name, only to hear Yashiro's call echo mine from the pier.

I ran up to Fujiki. "What happened to you?" I asked, hugely relieved.

"What happened to *you*, Shiomi? Where were you? I didn't know what to do."

"I was waiting for you in the quadrangle. Anyway, let's go."

"But, you see, Mori and the others want to take this boat across."

"Never mind them. Let's you and I walk."

Nevertheless, he continued across the beach and down to the water. I could only go with him, but not without a growing feeling of disappointment. He and I would never have our tête-à-tête if we were going by boat with a bunch of others.

"You really prefer the boat?"

"A while ago Mori and Ishii made me promise, I'm afraid."

"You made *me* a promise, too, though, didn't you?" A touch of anger had crept into my voice. He gave me a dejected look.

"I kept waiting for you, though, and you never came. I just didn't know what to do."

We were now close to the dock. "Hurry up, Fujiki!" This time it was Mori. The two figures—Yashiro midway along the dock, untying the mooring rope from the bollard, and Mori erect, swaying, in the boat—stood out against the sunset clouds.

"Fujiki, you're *really* going for the boat? You're no sailor, right? And look what a wind there is!"

"I'll be fine," he answered, his steps resounding on the dock.

I understood all too well the purpose evident in his receding figure. Even if we walked together to the village, his answer would be the same today as yesterday.

"What's going on? You went looking for Shiomi?" Yashiro's voice sounded teasing.

By now I was standing on the dock. From the boat, Mori blinked up at me. "Shiomi? Glad to have you!" he added.

"Why's that?" I asked.

Mori reached out to the dock and held the boat alongside while Fujiki, I, and Yashiro, in that order, stepped aboard. Yashiro took up his position in the stern and lowered the oar into the water. Mori leaned perilously forward and pushed against the bollard. The boat swayed and slid away.

"We were up for it, all right," said Mori, still standing in the bow, "but Yashiro said he felt we could do with another hand. Fujiki can't scull, after all."

"Hey now, I can do a *little* sculling!" Fujiki protested, putting up the collar of his cape.

Mori just laughed.

"Don't laugh!" I said. "It remains to be seen whether you and Yashiro can get us straight from here to the village! You have quite a breeze to contend with!"

"What do you mean? Arms of iron, nerves of steel, that's us!"

"I wonder. Didn't I see the two of you just going around and around in circles the other day?"

"You did not! That must have been a long time ago. We're getting better every day. Our coach was amazed!"

"Your coach? Who's that?"

"Kinoshita."

"Kinoshita, is it? Well, anyway, I just hope you know what you're doing."

"How about you, Shiomi?" Fujiki asked. "Are *you* any good at sculling?"

"About as good as Kinoshita, I suppose. I don't know about this wind, though. It's all different when there are waves."

Yashiro worked his oar in silence. For a while the boat glided along nicely, as long as the pines on the cape sheltered it from the strong westerly blowing in from the open ocean, but then waves began crashing against the side. The roaring pines on the cape swayed like a disaster warning, clouds spread over the sky, the last of the sunset light faded, and in no time darkness had swallowed the land.

"I can't see it!" Mori said.

"What?"

"Any boat ahead of us."

From the bow, Mori peered out across the waves. A few lights were twinkling off toward the village, but there wasn't a single boat on the bay. Around us you could see nothing but faintly glimmering breakers that foamed almost over the gunwale before they slid under the boat.

"That Ishii has a nerve!" Mori muttered to himself.

"What are you griping about?" I asked.

"He's just gone and left us here! Kinoshita's with him, too. Actually, we were all supposed to go together in the same boat, but then Fujiki disappeared, and so did Yashiro."

Yashiro spoke at last. "I was looking for Fujiki."

"I . . ." Fujiki turned toward me in evident dismay.

Yashiro's oar slipped off its pivot. While he lunged to grab it, the boat visibly changed direction.

"Watch out, there!" I called.

"I've had it, Shiomi! It's too much!"

"There you go, griping again!" Mori jumped up. "All right, *I'll* take it."

The wind had blown us a long way off course just in the short time no one had been sculling. Far from following a straight line from the point to our goal—the village wharf—the boat was now well on its way out toward the center of the bay. We'd thought the wind was from the west, which should have put it behind us, but now it seemed to be coming from the south. I half rose to my feet.

The boat rocked. Mori took the oar and shook his head at me.

"You're our trump card, Shiomi," he said. "Just wait till we need you."

I'd started to sit down again when a wave breaking against the side of the boat soaked me with spray. The exhausted Yashiro flopped down in front of me. With the towel I had at my waist I wiped the spray from my face. The wind felt strangely warm.

"How are you doing, Fujiki?" I asked.

"What do you mean?" He peered up into my face.

"This wind is bad!" Yashiro murmured with a worried look. He, too, was rubbing his face with a towel, although to wipe off spray or sweat I couldn't tell.

The oar popped off its pivot a second time, then a third. Each time the boat rolled and changed direction.

"You have to put your body into it more," I said. "Don't be shy about it. You'll never get anywhere unless you lean all the way forward."

"Right you are!"

Mori began sculling madly, but the boat went nowhere at all. In fact, I had the impression that the lights of the village were actually receding from us. My anxiety increased as the darkness grew. The wind howled its menace through the sky, and the boat creaked as though being slowly crushed.

Even the usually talkative Mori now plied the oar in grim silence. It was obviously hard work, and no wonder. In this part of the bay the inflowing tide collided with the southerly wind, raising peaked waves and creating complex currents. If the tide were now to turn, the wind might well drive us out into the open sea. One foreboding followed another.

"All right, I'll switch with you. You must be exhausted."

"I'll still be fine for a while."

Just as I moved to stand, Mori let out a sharp cry. While struggling to remain upright I saw his trousers fly up into the air like a

116

large, flapping bird. Then came a splash and a jet of spray, and only that cry remained behind.

"What happened?"

The three of us leaned over the side together, and the boat rocked violently. We were showered with spray.

"No!" I bawled, "Keep down! Don't stand up!"

Mori came straight back to the surface. I crawled to the stern and stretched an arm out to him. A wave washed over my hand.

"Come around here. You can't get back in over the side."

Mori's dripping hand gripped the stern board. Yashiro and Fujiki watched, both leaning against the gunwale on the same side, so that that side of the boat barely cleared the waves. I grasped Mori's hand to pull him up, but his soaking wet body was too heavy for me. Yashiro came to my aid.

"This is bad!"

Nonetheless, up Mori came and slid like a merman into the boat, dripping water everywhere.

"Get those clothes off! You'll catch cold!"

"I really flubbed that one. The oar rope broke."

"Quick!"

"I'm sorry!"

Mori hunched down and rapidly stripped. We rubbed him as well we could with the towel. Then Yashiro let out an agonized shout.

"What happened to the oar?"

It was pitch dark. The only light came from the sky. We must all have been pale with fear. Mori's teeth were chattering. We peered at the water, but there was no sign of anything like an oar.

"I really messed up, didn't I!" Mori threw his towel down at his feet and dove straight off the side before we could stop him, in only his drawers. After swimming just two or three strokes he vanished into the darkness.

"What a disaster! We've got to do something!"

I glanced back and saw Yashiro hurriedly undressing. He cut off my question to him.

"Shiomi, you stay here with Fujiki and keep watch. You'll have to keep shouting, though, or I'll lose the boat."

"Look, let *me* go."

"No, no, better me. I'm a good swimmer, I really am."

Despite my protests, Yashiro soon had his clothes off and calmly handed me his watch. Then he moistened his ears with his little finger and dove straight off the stern. He vanished from sight the opposite way from Mori. The darkness, blacker every moment, pressed down on the waves. Only their tops glimmered intermittently. The boat seemed to be drifting further and further off course.

"Shouldn't the moon be coming out?"

I peered hard at the watch Yashiro had handed me, but I couldn't see the hands. A lot of time must have already passed. Fujiki felt for my hand and moved beside me.

"The moon? It'll be up later than yesterday—somewhere after eight o'clock, I imagine."

"Right, and it's overcast, anyway. We're in trouble. I wonder whether they'll find it."

"Ishii and Kinoshita's boat must be there already."

"I suppose so."

Still, I cupped my hands into a megaphone and shouted twice, as loud as I could. The village lights twinkled over there, rising and sinking among the waves each time the boat rolled. My voice was lost in the engulfing darkness. The wind was so loud that there was no point in trying again. Instead I shifted direction to call out Mori and Yashiro's names, one after the other. This far out there was no phosphorescence. The waves absorbed the boat into their blackness.

"What if they don't find us?"

Fujiki's cold hand gripped mine. "They'll be all right," I muttered to make him feel better, but I had no idea how. Keep cool, keep cool, I told myself again and again. I no longer knew whether the wind was howling in the air or in my mind. I just kept praying for the moon to come out.

A splash, and before my eyes a hand gripped the gunwale.

"Any luck?"

"I couldn't find it." The voice was Mori's.

"Come up in the boat and take a rest. Yashiro's out there, too, looking. My turn next."

"But Shiomi," Mori answered with only his head above the waves, "it'll be all right if we do find it this way, but what if we don't? Wouldn't it be better just to swim back?"

"Back?"

"There was another boat still at the dock, and the old man who gives us our meals is there, too. Shouldn't we take it, then, and try again?"

"But we can't do *that*! It's quite a way, back to the dock."

I gazed across the waves toward the point. A faint light showed through the torn clouds to the west, just bright enough for me to make out the pinewood. Off toward the dormitory a single light was burning.

"It's so far, though, and with these waves . . ."

"No, it's not too far to swim. If we don't do something fast we'll be swept out to sea. Besides, this is all my fault."

"Don't be silly!"

Yashiro's voice came next, from the stern.

"Go back? That might be the best thing to do. All right, I'll go."

"Oh no you don't!" Mori barked. "This one's for *me*."

"I don't know about you, Mori. I may not look like much, but I was in the swimming club in middle school. Besides, if *you* go, you may not be able to do much for us once you get there."

"You jerk, I'll get you for that!"

Mori looked up at me. "Just wait here, Shiomi, please," he said, released the gunwale, and swiftly disappeared toward the point.

"Wait! Wait!" Yashiro called after him. "Damn, he's gone! Shiomi, I'm going, too. It'll be safer that way. He'd never be able to scull a boat all the way back here. You won't mind waiting here? You're all right, aren't you, Fujiki? Shiomi, look after him for me."

He vanished into the darkness without another word.

"You can see the light in the lodge," I bellowed toward him. "You've got to keep to the left of it! Keep to the left! You have to make absolutely sure you're not carried out further into the bay! Swim together!"

No answer came back. Fujiki was gripping my arm hard.

"They're gone," I murmured.

The wind seemed to be dropping a little. The waves were still high, but perhaps not quite what they'd been before. The boat, with just the two of us in it, continued its wild tossing and writhing. The sky began to clear. A sort of dim radiance to the east announced moonrise.

Fujiki and I crouched, hand in hand, in the stern. Bleak thoughts whirled through my head. This dinky little boat wouldn't last long if we ended up being blown out of the bay and into the open sea. Mori and Yashiro were unlikely to get back in time, even if they actually made it to the dock in the first place. I bitterly regretted having foolishly let them go. The one to go should have been me.

"I'm sure they'll be all right, those two."

No trace of their passage remained on the dark sea. "Well, at least there isn't much chance of a shark getting them," I murmured. For us, there was nothing to do but wait. Whether or not we'd be saved depended entirely on the others.

"Fujiki, I'm going to look for that oar. It's not doing us any good to sit around waiting like this."

"No! Don't go!" Fujiki spoke with unusual conviction and urgency. He seized my arm.

"Why? I may actually find it."

"But . . . No, let's just stay like this."

He moved even closer, and I felt his warmth. His hand was slippery with sweat.

"You're afraid?" I asked gently.

"Not for me, no. For you."

Fujiki brought his face close to mine. I smelled a sort of faint sweetness.

"I'm sorry, Shiomi."

"What about?"

"I'm the one who got you into this. If I hadn't wanted you to come . . ."

"It's all right, I promise. Don't worry about it. Actually . . ."

Actually, I was happy. The thought echoed through me like an orchestral *fortissimo*. My fear receded, and being alone like this with Fujiki, drifting helplessly over the sea, made me happier than I had ever dreamed of being.

"I feel really bad about this, Shiomi," he repeated.

"I do want to go and look for that oar. I think I'd better."

"Forget about it. It's no use any more. Let's just stay like this instead. Let's just wait."

"If that's what you want . . ."

Could this mean that Fujiki loved me? His preferring to stay like this, hand in hand with me while we waited in this oarless boat—surely, surely this meant that he loved me! Preferring just to stay together, gauging the weight of our fear . . . I put my arm around his slim body and drew him closer.

That familiar dazzle, that sort of dizzy rapture, filled my whole being. I no longer had any thought for Mori or Yashiro. Fujiki and I were alone in the world, with nothing around us—no sky, no sea, no space, no time. Wind might blow, waves might roar, but this night, this love, were eternity. All fear, all despair was gone. Taut skin tingling with love for the figure in my arms, I knew at last the extraordinary feeling of being loved, tasted that soaring, swooning sensation, experienced in oneness of spirit and body the utter rightness of embracing him, and only prayed that this intoxication might last forever.

"Ah, here comes the moon!"

Fujiki's voice thrilled me to the core. I opened my eyes. A round moon, just past the full, was rising from the mountain ridge that towered darkly behind the scattered lights of the village. The wind had cleared most of the clouds from the sky, leaving only broken wisps that trailed, white in the moonlight, about the mountain's slopes.

We then wandered anew a dreamlike realm. We saw now that we were alone in the middle of the bay, surrounded by foaming waves and drifting slowly away from the village. The encircling houses, the point, and the cliffs loomed far off, silent in the wind. The view floated beyond space and time, and there on the moonlit sea we became pure spirit.

This is love, I wanted to tell him, and I was sure he'd now understand. The words wouldn't come to my lips, though; instead I just gazed entranced at his face, pale in the moonlight—the black eyes, like brimming pools beneath a forest of long lashes; the pupils glowing like pearls; the fine, smooth bridge of the Grecian nose; the fine, slightly parted lips; and the subtle harmony with which the Creator had endowed all these features.

But, the word "love" always aroused an uneasiness that now, with its discordant note, began to dispel my intoxication. There is anguish in the presence of things too beautiful, too pure. Then I noticed, amid the slap of waves against the side, the noise of water also at my feet. Water was sloshing around in the bottom of the boat. It *couldn't* have sprung a leak, though! I noted again the dark, unsightly tangle of clothes that Mori and Yashiro had left behind. I remembered Yashiro's parting words—"Shiomi, look after him for me."—and pondered their significance.

At some point the boat had changed direction, and the moon now shone down on us from a different angle. Fujiki shivered.

"What the matter? Are you afraid?"

He looked right at me. The moonlight cut his face vertically into two halves, bright and dark.

"Why do you ask?"

He smiled a little. White teeth gleamed between his lips. His trusting, dreamy expression contrasted with my apprehension. Every instrument in the orchestra of emotion struck a new note, and the symphony rose to a *tutti*. To love means to trust, to live each moment without regret! What does "fear" mean? Death—what's that? This peace deep in the soul, this pure joy, this music, this moonlight . . . I could die happy now, just like this, loving you, this very moment . . . So ran my thoughts, and I had only to speak them.

"Shiomi, what's that over there?"

His excited voice brought me back to reality. He was pointing out over the waves. The moon was already well up in the sky.

"Hey, isn't that our oar?"

I peered as hard as I could. It really did look like an oar. I began stripping off my jacket.

"You're going in, Shiomi?"

"Of course I am. This is great! What fantastic luck!"

"You'll be all right?"

"I'll be fine. It's right there, isn't it?"

Fujiki gave a worried frown. I dove straight into the water.

Once the first shock of cold was past, the water turned out to be quite warm, and the waves, now I was in among them, were not really as rough as all that. I began swimming in the general direction of the oar.

"To the right, more to the right!" Fujiki shouted.

I returned to the boat, thrusting the oar in front of me. Fujiki leaned far out over the side to retrieve it.

"You'll get soaked," I said. "I'll lift it into the boat afterwards."

"I don't mind," Fujiki replied gravely. He'd already taken off his cape.

I clambered back in over the stern and found myself shivering. "Are you cold?" Fujiki asked, rubbing my back with a towel. He kept at it for some time.

"I'm glad you're back. I was worried."

"Why? You needn't have been. It wasn't far, was it?"

"I was afraid there might be sharks around."

"Not a chance. You really believe there could be sharks in a place like this?"

"But, Shiomi, didn't you tell those two a while ago that you hoped the sharks wouldn't get them?"

"I never said anything of the kind!"

My mood was cheerful, but I couldn't help noticing that the spell was broken. I felt a sort of selfish regret.

I put my clothes back on, tore the towel in two, tied the ends together, and made an oar rope of it. Then I put the oar in the water, planted my feet firmly, and thrust hard against it. The boat creaked and turned halfway around, as though alive again. I began sculling with short strokes.

All that time soaking in the water had made the oar heavy to work. I could soon feel sweat on my forehead, but the boat slid surprisingly smoothly over the waves. The moonlight grew brighter, and the white, broken clouds glided northward along the sky. As my arms tired, the thought of Mori and Yashiro, and their swim back to shore, worried me more and more. I pushed my arms harder with every grim vision that floated into my mind. Fujiki shouted toward the point. Several voices echoed his in reply. At last I made out several figures standing on the dock, stopped sculling, and shouted in turn.

"Are Mori and Yashiro with you?"

The answer came from close by.

"Don't worry, they're safe."

A boat I hadn't noticed before was there right beside us. I'd just recognized Kinoshita's voice when it bumped into us. "Thank heavens, thank heavens!" Yanai stammered as he jumped into our boat. "All right, take a rest."

"Sorry to have worried you all like this."

"What are you talking about? We should've sent a boat after you long ago."

We soon reached the dock. The first-year students surrounded Fujiki and accompanied him to where Mori and Yashiro were waiting beside a fire. I left it to Kinoshita to tidy up the boat and walked off along the beach among a knot of others, giving them an account of the evening's events. "You look pretty happy, though," said Hattori teasingly.

The day before the camp was to close, we gave up the afternoon archery session in order to pack. Then, during the hours left until dinnertime, we went for a walk through the tangerine orchard.

The orchard, just behind our lodge, grew on a sunny, southern slope facing the sea. A twisting hillside trail took us up to where golden tangerines glowed among green leaves on heavily burdened branches. We could easily have eaten our fill, but these were sour, summer tangerines, and we weren't that hungry. They puckered up your mouth till you made a face. Still, all the leaves rustled when you picked a big one from its branch, and it left a fine spray on your face when you sank a nail into the golden rind. That fresh sensation never palled on us, there in the spring sunshine and the soft sea breeze.

Fujiki and I sat down together under a tree that afforded a good view. Over our heads drooped tangerine-laden branches, while voices droned on sleepily in the distance. The sun was sinking toward the west, and backlit clouds hung on the horizon like a white curtain. Below us the cliff dropped away to a vast expanse of sea. Low waves crept turtle-like across it, glittering in the sun. "They look like an unbroken sheet of benzene nuclei," he murmured to himself. We each lazily peeled a tangerine and dropped its sections into our mouths.

"That other evening when we were out there," I asked, "weren't you afraid?"

"Hmm." He thought about it a while. "No, not especially."

"How well can you swim, anyway?"

"I can't swim at all." He laughed.

"What? You can't? I don't believe it! You've really got guts!"

"I'm hopeless at it."

"Then you *must* have been afraid. Didn't you think you might die?"

"Yes, I did. I wasn't afraid, though."

"But look," I pressed him with an irony inspired by our closeness, "you tried to stop me, didn't you, when I went to get the oar?"

"I wanted to be with you then."

"Why?"

"I thought I might die, and I felt I might be able to love you if I died that way."

"So it's no good any more, now?"

"Now? Now I'm alive, and I can't see the need to love anyone."

"It was just that one evening, then?"

"Yes. I suppose it's because I was sure I was going to die. It'd be so miserable to die alone."

Fujiki stared down at the sea with the sweet, melancholy look that was typical of him.

Cupid must have already fluttered off by then, on his little wings, and I just hadn't noticed. I gazed at his profile and convinced myself that the sense of beauty it conveyed was more spiritual in nature than *physique*. Love transcending death, love of the kind I'd known while we drifted over the moonlit sea, could never again sound its unearthly note. Loving that spirit meant loving this profile, this slight, fleshly body. There was no contradiction involved. Just as I loved Fujiki, Fujiki—yes, Fujiki—did love me: that thought alone brought boundless happiness.

The next day, all of us at the camp were to walk from Toi over Nanmyō Pass to Yugashima, where we'd spend the night before returning to Tokyo. I looked forward to making the journey over the mountains with Fujiki, and I explained the planned route to him. He listened, nodding occasionally.

Few people were left in the dining hall by the time we got back to the lodge, and the festive Satsuma stew was cold. We ate our meal sitting across the table from each other, in the dim light of the bare electric bulb. Just then Yashiro rushed into the room.

"Fujiki, it's a telegram! It just came!"

Fujiki went pale and opened it. Panting, Yashiro peered at it from the side.

"What is it?" I asked, chopsticks still in hand.

"It's from Chieko. Mother's sick, and she wants me to come home."

"I wonder what's the matter. Is it a sudden illness?"

"Oh, it's just a cold or something." Fujiki showed no sign of being especially worried. "Chieko wants me there because she's lonely."

"If that's all it is, then fine."

"Chieko always needs me when something happens," he complained mildly. Still, he didn't look too happy.

"So you're going right away?" Yashiro asked.

"Yes."

"Will you make it?"

Yashiro glanced at his watch. The last launch for Numazu had already left. "You'll have to take the first one tomorrow," I said. Fujiki gave an unenthusiastic response and got back to his meal.

"The first one's at six thirty, right? What are you going to do? Walk to the village?"

"Sure, I only have one bag."

"I could take you by boat."

"No thanks," he said with a little laugh, "I've had my fill of boats. Anyway, you needn't see me off at all. You have a fair way to walk tomorrow. You'll get too tired."

"I see."

"So much for our plan to cross the mountains together. I'm really sorry."

"That's all right. It's not *that* important. What does matter is this. After all, Chieko knows you're due back late on the day after tomorrow."

"Chieko's a scaredy-cat. My mother is fine. There's nothing much to worry about."

We lingered there, talking, even after we'd finished our meal. I decided that instead of seeing Fujiki off to the village, I'd wave him good-bye from the tip of the promontory. "That won't be much fun for you," Fujiki remarked, looking a bit gloomy himself.

"Come to think of it, weren't *you* out there once, right at the tip?"

"At the tip?" He gave me an odd look. "Yes, I went there a lot."

"A lot? To a deserted spot like that?"

"I did a lot of thinking there. How did you find out, Shiomi?"

"I once took a walk out there. I saw you and called, but you mustn't have heard me. The place is so desolate somehow—it's really depressing."

"You think so? *I* don't."

"Why's that?"

"Why? Well, it's the same wherever you are. You're always lonely."

He looked at me vacantly, as though staring off into some invisible distance.

The sound of dripping invaded my dreams. I opened my eyes to see moisture on the window and rain fogging the air outside. The room smelled of mold. Yanai and Kinoshita, still in bed, were whispering to each other.

"Why did it just *have* to rain today?"

"Ah, Yanai, you poor fellow, you have no poetry in you. 'Spring rain—just enough to get the little beach shells wet'—you know who wrote that?"

"That kind of stuff's not my line. It's no fun at all, though, walking in the rain."

"Oh, it'll stop soon enough. I've been praying for fine weather."

I glanced at the clock, got up, and quickly began to dress. Then I folded my bedding, grabbed my cap, and was on my way out the door when Tachibana, who I'd assumed was asleep, suddenly called out to me. "Don't forget your cape, Shiomi," he said. "You'll get wet."

Without a word I took the thing from its peg on the wall and left the room feeling three pairs of eyes boring into my back. Tachibana could never keep a secret, so even Yanai and Kinoshita knew by now that I was on my way to wave good-bye to Fujiki. His unfailing concern had succeeded only in annoying me, and that annoyance clouded my mood all the way to the tip of the cape.

And there I waited, straining my ears, until I made out through the rhythmic noise of the waves the chug of the approaching motor. The boat's whistle pierced the morning calm, and in no time the boat itself glided into view. The black hull sliced through the waves, and there was Fujiki, leaning on the deck railing, behind him a scattering of cargo and a pair of men squatting down in rubber rain gear. White steam burst from the pipe next to the engine room as the whistle sounded again.

Fujiki's gaze, cool and lonely as ever, was on me. Light gleamed faintly in his eyes as the launch passed before me out into the open sea. Then the rudder swung it to the right, and Fujiki's black cape dwindled gradually from view. That was all. This brief parting had given me nothing but a glance from Fujiki and that light in his eyes. I lowered my hand, wet with rain. Then happiness flooded through me, heightened by the smell of the shore, the charm of the spring buds, and the salt breeze lazily wafting through countless raindrops. Fujiki is gone, but Fujiki is here, here within me, always with me . . .

I jumped down from the top of my rock. The boat was just a dot by now on the horizon, and then even that dot disappeared. After a last look I put up the collar of my cape and started back cheerfully through the rain.

The Second Notebook

Fujiki Chieko: the girl I loved in my youth.

I close my eyes and try to picture Chieko at twenty, when I was closest to her. But what I remember refuses to coalesce into a single, clear image. Sometimes I get only vague impressions superimposed on one another. Is my memory failing, then? This girl is the only woman I've ever loved, and yet I can't exactly remember her face. There must be some reason for that.

Fujiki Chieko wasn't especially pretty. Back when I was close to her brother, I often wished that she looked more like him. She was a perfectly ordinary girl student, the kind you see anywhere, except that her eyes were always clear and sparkling with intelligence. Her expression, though, changed constantly with her mood, hardly ever conveying a single, settled emotion. In disposition she was sunny, guileless, in fact distinctly vivacious. Perhaps I saw intelligence in her eyes only because she was studying in the mathematics department of a women's university. But to fall in love you don't necessarily have to find yourself a beauty. For me as I was then, always gloomy and withdrawn, with few friends and hardly any family, this healthy, cheerful girl became my dream. With my habitually fantastic imagination I saw her sometimes as Dante's Beatrice, sometimes as Petrarch's Laura. Just as her ever-changing expression eluded definition, I likened her in my fantasies to one beauty after another, loving her now as Chloe, now as Isolde. In short, she represented for me not one face but, rather, a variety of women who inspired my artistic yearnings. On reflection, she did perhaps actually somewhat resemble the young Countess Anna de Noailles. Round face and bright eyes, fine, gentle lips, and full cheeks—my impression of her probably corresponded subtly to the feminine image that I already harbored deep within me.

Another reason why I can't precisely recall her face must have to do with how rapidly she was maturing and how quickly time passed for us then. When I met her, on my first visit to the Fujikis' house, her brother had just started high school, and she herself had only just entered a girls' school. As a result, she was only a third-year student in the same school when her brother suddenly died. I ended up making frequent visits to this bereaved family, reduced now to just mother and daughter, perhaps because I felt it was my duty to look after this young girl in her brother's stead. Fujiki Shinobu's classmates Yashiro, Mori, and Ishii, too, took turns visiting the family, but I went more often than they did. Being a lonely college student, I also went for the family's comforting warmth. Fujiki's mother was naturally cheerful, and although she would probably never quite get over losing her beloved son, her gracious hospitality never failed. Chieko, like her, was never shy or taciturn. The three of us had a good time together. I'd lost my mother in childhood, and in my hometown I had only a brother utterly different in age. I'd never had a sister, and I was able to feel closer to this mother and daughter than to anyone else.

Meanwhile, Chieko gradually grew up. I accompanied her to the entrance exam for her women's university, and it's about then that this childlike, innocent girl began to awaken to herself as a young woman. We debated things quite freely, and when she lost and began to cry, her trembling lips were not a child's. We didn't always get on especially well. She was a Christian. Moreover, Yashiro and Ishii, among others, were studying around this time with the Non-Church Christian leader Sawada, and it's probably under their influence that she, too, became interested in the movement. There were many issues on which she was bound to disagree with someone like me, who was studying ancient languages and aimed to be a writer. For me, there was nothing to believe in and no God. When I told her it was absurd for a mathematics major to believe in God, she retorted, for example, that the ultimate goal of science is to perceive the divine. She was in deadly earnest then, and her eyes shone. When I conceded defeat a mischievous glint would come into her eyes, and she'd clear her throat with an ostentatious "Ahem!" Then she and her mother would have a good laugh.

I graduated from college and, failing to find a job I wanted, fell back on my knowledge of Italian to go to work for an organization involved with Italian culture. I returned to my hometown to undergo my military induction exam and was declared a grade B first-class reservist. The war broke out a year later, and most of my friends went off, one by one, into the army. Anxiety about when I might receive my own draft notice, in its red envelope, gradually shaped the character of my feelings for Fujiki Chieko.

There on the traffic island, hands in my overcoat pockets, I let three Hongō-bound streetcars go by. I looked around me. People were strolling down the Ginza sidewalk as though they'd never heard of war anywhere in the world. A dazzle of light gleamed from the shop windows, and the constant stream of passing cars seemed to wash me with the brilliance of their headlights. Up there, the clock on the Hattori tower showed nine o'clock, but I still couldn't make up my mind. Instead I plunged unsteadily into the throng and walked on toward Yūraku-chō.

I'd been drinking with friends at the München beer hall until a short time ago; then I'd left early, saying I was going home. While waiting for a streetcar at the 4-chōme corner I remembered the book of Petrarch's poetry left open on the desk in my room. My practice was to read a sonnet a day, and I still hadn't read today's. I also had to get to work on the novel I kept planning to write. But, despite these stirrings of conscience, I felt a growing desire to go and see Chieko. Perhaps the late spring chill and the fumes of drink had something to do with it. At Yūraku-chō I boarded a commuter train, whispering to myself that, after all, the long-vanished Laura was no concern of mine.

After Fujiki Shinobu's death, his mother and sister had moved to a rented apartment near Ōmori Station, on a height overlooking the sea. My heart swelled with anticipation, as always, when I got off the train and climbed the slope away from the broad avenue. The street was dark, the neighborhood silent. Trees spread their branches into the road over the concrete walls. Walking at a leisurely pace, I checked my watch by the dim light of a streetlamp. It was late, all right. I intentionally blamed my drinking for wanting to go and see her face at so late an hour.

I climbed the stairs to the second floor of the building and rang the doorbell briefly twice. The door opened immediately.

"Goodness, Shiomi-san, it's you! I didn't think it sounded like Mother."

"She's not here?"

"Come in, come in. She's off chatting with some neighbors. She'll be back soon."

I took off my shoes and, still standing in the entrance, asked for a drink of water. Then I went on into the south-facing six-mat room, the second of the apartment's two rooms.

"I'll put some tea on."

"No thanks, just water."

"Well, well! Fancy that!" she said, suppressing her merriment.

"Fancy what? I'm just the usual me."

"No, you're not."

Chieko went into the kitchen. A box containing the funerary urn stood on a small cupboard in the corner, with before it a framed photograph of her brother in his student uniform. I took off my coat on the tatami, knelt in front of the photo, and bowed.

"Here you are!"

I drained in one breath the glass of cold water she gave me.

"You shouldn't stare at people that way."

"How much did you drink? A lot?"

"Just a little. I'm sober now."

"So did you get any inspiration?"

"Yes, I was inspired to come and see you."

"You're hopeless."

Chieko plumped down at the desk but made no attempt to read the book that lay open on it. Instead she went on with her questions.

"What's the point of drinking, anyway? Do you get more work done when you drink?"

"I don't drink that much, you know. It has nothing to do with work."

"But don't all novelists drink? That book you told me to read a while ago, it's full of degenerate characters."

"Oh, that?" I laughed. "The author's sometimes interested in such cases. That's all. I have no wish to imitate him."

"You did say, though, didn't you, that you greatly admire him."

"I certainly did. He's a highly original novelist, an uncompromising individual who insists on being himself. I don't feel in the least like mimicking his life by wandering around Tamanoi.[1] On the whole, I have no intention of writing my private life into my work. His books *are* fascinating, though—a blend of cultural critique in which he figures as a sort of *étranger*, and of lyrical writing permeated by a thoroughly Japanese feeling for the seasons. Anyway, he's an exceptional writer. You just can't lump him to-

---

1   The book in question seems to be *Bokutō Kitan* (Strange Tale from East of the River, 1937) by Nagai Kafū (1879–1959). Tamanoi was a cheap, popular quarter east of the Sumida River, inhabited by many unlicensed prostitutes.

gether with the usual scribblers."

"Oh no, even I agree he's better than that. Still, an artist's work reflects his life, don't you think?"

"Certainly."

"Which means he'd never manage to write anything worthwhile if he didn't live a depraved a life himself . . ."

"No, no, that's not true."

"Why? Does your admiration extend even to a life like that?"

"What I mean is *not* that he has to live like that to write something good. You can draw superior work from any kind of life at all."

"Really? As far as I can see, that's clearly the life he prefers. He's getting on now, but he's still a bachelor, and he goes off to amuse himself with women whenever he feels like it. Right? Now, *you're* a bachelor too . . . Oh dear, the water's boiling!"

Chieko nimbly rose and dashed to the kitchen. With a sour look I racked my brains for arguments to prove my case. Chieko didn't trust novelists, and she took it for granted that they led seedy lives.

She returned with cups of black tea.

"So when are you going to write your masterpiece?" she asked, shifting the conversation in a new direction.

"Me? Oh, pretty soon now!" I grinned.

"But what *kind* of novel are you going to write? A love story?"

"Well, I know there'll be a girl like you in it."

"Oh no! And you just said you didn't plan to draw on your private life!"

"No, you see, it's not like that. I certainly don't plan to model a character directly on you. It's more that I have my own, personal image for my character, and it's based on you. It has to do with the beauty of youth, or something like that, raised to a universal level. That's the image I mean to write about."

"In other words . . . well, it's just a dream."

"What's wrong with that? That's the way I live. I go to work every day and write perfectly ordinary letters and so on in Italian, but the real me is the one who goes home again to his room and reads Petrarch. Petrarch is where I find my dreams. Reading Theocritus and Catullus is what makes life worth living. I don't understand what people call reality. This war that's going on—it makes no sense to me. The very thought of being drafted horrifies me, but I haven't the strength either to oppose the war or to stop it. All I can do under the circumstances is to evade the situation and be free at least within myself, unhindered by the war. Really, I have nothing of my own but my dreams. What I want is to enter fully into the world of the classics and see again there, with my own eyes, the dreams that the poets have dreamed.

"Isn't that being a bit of a coward, though?" Chieko looked down as she quietly stirred her tea with her spoon.

"A coward? Why?"

"Well, the classics aren't the world we live in."

"Of course not. That's why I don't bury myself in musty old books to become a scholar of classical literature. I want to be a novelist."

"These novels of yours, though—they're like dreams too, aren't they?"

"I write for myself. Literary schools or the trends of the times have nothing to do with it. Naturally I can't be sure I'll ever be published, but I'll be glad enough just to satisfy myself."

"And the war?"

"External reality doesn't concern me. Internal reality is all that matters. Look, I won't be able to talk like this once I'm drafted, and I don't even know when that will be. So I'd like to use the time I have till then in the way most congenial to me, the way that'll leave me with the fewest regrets."

"I understand that, but still . . ."

Chieko had been toying with her spoon (I'd noticed some time ago how much like her brother she was in her movements), but now she suddenly stood up and went to the window. She opened it, sat down on the ledge below it, and gazed out into the night.

I went up to her. The distant sea remained invisible under the dark sky, but the shopping street lights along the railroad tracks burned brightly. The odor of the trees filled the clear air.

"What's the matter?" I asked.

"Nothing," she murmured. That was all. I put my hands on her shoulders.

"You just please yourself, don't you?" she said.

"Why do you say that?"

"Because all these things you have in your head, all your classics and your literature, have nothing whatever to do with *us*."

"What I have in my head is mostly you, Chieko."

"All right, but the Chieko you mean lives only in your head. She isn't *me*."

"Nonsense!"

A train heading out from Tokyo rumbled past, its line of windows flashing.

"Shiomi-san, I'm sure you can be a great novelist, or anything else you like, but I'm not what you want."

"What on earth do you mean?"

She slowly raised her head to look up at me. The sorrow in her expression stood out all the more clearly because she was normally so animated.

"I can't be what you've been talking about."

"Why? I'm not asking you to be anything special. You're fine just as you are. That's the Chieko I love."

"You're a dreamer. Yes, a dreamer. You were dreaming, too, when you loved my brother. I'll never forget his words. 'Shiomi's dreaming,' he said, 'but I can't share his dream.' No, and nor can I. I'm his sister, after all."

"But, Chieko, I'm not asking you to dream anything! Don't you understand?"

"All right, you'll wake up eventually, and the dream will be gone. I don't want to end up abandoned."

Chieko turned again toward the night, her thin lips quivering. Her profile suddenly struck me as uncannily like her brother's. Am I really that much of a dreamer? I wondered. Is it really so bad to dream?

"It isn't the same any more," I said slowly, my hands still on her shoulders. "Back then I was young, too, and I knew nothing whatever about the world. I was just living for all I was worth, and that's what I thought life was. There'd be no hatred, no cruelty, no inhumanity, I thought—no, all would be well if only there was love. It's not like that now. Now I understand all too clearly that my own world and the world outside me are completely different. Here we are, hounded by war, yet who among us has ever really wanted war? Who on earth would gladly fight this barbarous, ignorant, inhuman war? But we're all completely helpless, and there's absolutely nothing we can do when the red draft envelope finally comes. I can't stand it. That's why, at least for now, I just want to be myself and express my dreams. You might say that if I dream now, it's because I do so deliberately, not because, as in the old days, dreaming is the only way I know to live. I know perfectly well that there are many ways of living. It's just that this is the one I've chosen for myself. Do you see what I mean?"

"Yes, I do." Her voice was low. "But . . ."

"But what? Say it!"

"But doesn't living like that just lead to unhappiness?"

"Unhappiness? You're bound to be unhappy anyway. Where in the world are you going to find happiness? You graduate from college, and there's war waiting for you. And what awaits you after war is probably death. You live in fear day after day, and somewhere along the line you give up what you really are to act big and brave . . . And where does that get you? Don't you agree, Chieko?"

"But I have my faith, you see." I could barely hear her.

An inbound train, then immediately an outbound one, crossed in a shower of bright sparks and a blaze of lighted windows. We watched them in silence. Abruptly Chieko shrugged her shoulders and stood up. A voice at the entrance had called, "I'm home!"

"Welcome back! Shiomi-san is here."

"I got to talking. My, my, good evening!"

I'd sat down in Chieko's place on the ledge below the window, looking glum, and from there I watched mother and daughter enter the room. Chieko's face showed no sign of her recent dejection.

"Do come in here! Aren't you cold, with the window open?"

"Not especially." I sat down cross-legged on the tatami, leaning against the window. "How are you, Mrs. Fujiki?" I asked.

"I'm fine, thank you. I spend my time quarreling with Chieko."

"I'll go and put on some water." Chieko stood up.

"No, it's getting late. I'd better be going."

"Oh, don't go so soon. Isn't there something we can offer him?" she asked Chieko.

"I'm fine, really," I said. "What do you quarrel about?"

She smiled indulgently. "Chieko keeps urging me to read the Bible and go to lectures with her. She's a bit of a pest on the subject. I doubt it would do me much good by now."

"Oh, is *that* it?" I laughed.

The sliding door opened, and in came Chieko bearing an orange on a plate. "There was just this one," she said. Then, turning to me, "Is something funny?"

"You're trying to convert your mother, are you?"

"Well, it's nothing to laugh about!"

"What's your religion, Mrs. Fujiki?"

"Oh, I'm an agnostic. My family are Pure Land Buddhists, though. I was terribly upset when Shinobu died, but lately I'm happy to say . . ."

"Mother, faith isn't just for leaning on God when you're in trouble. Everyday life is what matters."

"Yes, yes, Chieko, whatever you say."

I laughed and put a section of the orange Chieko had divided in my mouth. Chieko glared at me angrily.

"You're being flippant, Shiomi-san. I don't like it."

"No, I'm not. Even I think about such things."

"Thinking gets you nowhere. You have to believe."

"It's not that simple. Won't you have some, Chieko?"

"Not with you playing games with me this way, no!"

Nonetheless, she deftly took a piece of orange. The orange was soon gone. "I'll bring something next time," I said.

Chieko's mother watched us, smiling. "I wonder whether the water's boiling yet," she said and got up.

"I'm really going."

"Jumpy, aren't you?" Chieko was glaring at me again.

"Come to think of it, Chieko, would you like to go to a concert next Saturday evening?"

"Goodness me!" She rolled her eyes. "*That's* a surprise! You're an odd one, you are."

"There's nothing odd about it. It had just slipped my mind till this minute."

"What's the program?"

"It's the Shinkyō Orchestra. They're doing Chopin's first piano concerto. Let's go! It's a wonderful piece."

"Mother!" Chieko called toward the kitchen. She sounded excited.

"Is it all right if I go?" she asked, before her mother had even brought in the tea things.

"What's this about?" Her mother calmly sat down and began pouring the tea.

"It's for Saturday evening, a concert. I can go, can't I?"

"Mr. Shiomi is so busy, though."

"No, it's fine. I really want to go, and if it's all right for Chieko . . ."

"I'd like to go, Mother, I really would."

Her mother finished pouring. "You didn't pester him to invite you, did you?" There was a touch of severity in her voice.

We descended the stone steps of the concert hall. The subdued crowd was beginning to disperse into scattered, shadowy little clusters of people. The air was warm and heavy, as though with the lingering reverberations of the music. We walked along at a leisurely pace, savoring our fading impressions of what we'd heard. It felt as though we couldn't possibly walk slowly enough.

"How about some tea, Chieko?"

She turned toward me and shook her head.

"It seems you don't want to talk," I teased her.

"It was so beautiful, though. Didn't it affect you that much?"

"Of course it did. Concerts are really my only pleasure."

"What about me, then?" she asked mischievously.

"Oh dear, you got me. Of course I love being with you, Chieko. But seeing you also brings painful things to mind: Christianity, the war, and so on—anything that affects our relationship. Listening to music has no painful associations. My heart's full, and I can dream as much as I like. I feel as though I'm really living. Isn't it like that for you?"

"I don't hear music that often. It *was* wonderful this evening, though—just wonderful."

"Why were you so eager to go? Most of the time you have trouble making up your mind to accept an invitation."

"I wanted to hear Chopin. I'm mad about Chopin. You know all about music, though—does that seem funny to you?"

"Not at all. Anyway, I certainly *don't* know all about music."

"One of my classmate friends is fond of music, but she has no use for Chopin—she says he's too sweet. Maybe she's right."

"Sweet or not, that's not the issue. The right music for each of us is the music that moves us most deeply. Chopin may be sweet, but he gave his whole life to writing music. He only barely managed to get it written down, too. He had TB, so he probably knew he didn't have that long to live. It must be awful to know you're going to die."

"Stop thinking like that!"

"All right. But to me, no healthy person should look down on Chopin for being sweet. For that matter, all artists bear something like a burden of pain and live expecting to collapse at any moment."

"This is too depressing! I don't want to hear any more!"

"Me, I still want to be an artist, but my real work lies in the future, and in the meantime, with this war going on, I don't know how long I have. The greatness of Chopin's artistic achievement is inimitable—just extraordinary. That's the kind of thing I'd like to achieve, too. I have to admit that I'm better off than Chopin, since even if I do go into the army, I'm still not sure I'll die."

"That's right. I don't want you to die. Enough of this!"

I nodded, mumbled assent, and walked cautiously on, my hands in my pockets. Chieko walked beside me, her slight figure brushing against me. We took a dim side street. I thought how lovely it would be if only she and I, just the two of us, could walk on this way forever. But we soon reached the streetcar stop.

We boarded the commuter train at Shinbashi and stood side by side, hanging onto the leather straps and swaying with the movement of the train. Sometimes our shoulders touched.

Whenever they did, the astonishing melody of the concerto we'd just heard, and the piano's glittering notes, would swell within me like a harbinger of bliss. The buzz of voices in the packed carriage and the grubby carriage itself then vanished, and it felt as though just the two of us were swaying toward happiness on infinitely recurring waves of music. Softly, reverently, I whistled the tune. Chieko glanced toward me, her eyes brimming with shared feeling.

The mood continued even after we'd left the train. When we started up the dark slope I drew one hand from my pocket and put my arm around her shoulders. Her slender shoulders meekly leaned into me.

"Shiomi-san," she said, "a while ago you exclaimed, 'Happiness? Where are you going to find *that*?' Didn't you?"

"I suppose I did."

"Yes. There's no such thing as happiness, you said. But aren't you happy now?"

"Yes, I am. And you?"

"Me, too."

She spoke in a whisper, with downcast eyes so that I couldn't see her expression. I stopped, drew her closer, and gently turned her to face me. The weak streetlamp shed only a dim light on her face, which looked caught in eternity. Faint embarrassment glazed it, as though with thin ice. The piano harmonies still floated through my mind.

I brought my face close to hers, but she gently pressed her hands to my chest.

"We mustn't."

"Why?"

Chieko shook her head, looking more embarrassed than ever. "Let's keep walking," she said in a low voice.

I, too, was suddenly embarrassed. In the past Chieko had never allowed me to kiss her. "I don't like doing things like that," she'd say, and if I insisted at all she'd go on in a girlish tone, "I *do* love you, though—isn't that enough?" The memory of those moments came back to me. We started walking again, and I suddenly became talkative.

"Every *phrase* of Chopin's music is his alone. Of course that's true of every composer—Mozart always sounds like Mozart or Schumann like Schumann—but especially in Chopin's case, those dreamlike melodies have a unique beauty that runs through the whole piece. In a truly original work a melody like that may seem to appear repeatedly, but it's never really the same when it does so. Each recurrence is subtly different, and sometimes the difference is very bold, but the result is always pure Chopin. That's why, if the piece is his, a single phrase tells you it's by him. There's no mistaking him for anyone else."

"You *do* know a lot about music, don't you?" There was a hint of irony in her voice.

"No, honestly, I don't. Don't take me too seriously."

"You really love music, though. Which do you love more, music or literature?"

"What I want is to write literature that's like music. That might sound a bit contradictory, but I think it would be wonderful to merge the elements of music freely into one's writing."

"By writing you mean poetry, I suppose?"

"Yes, poetry is the closest literary genre to music. I don't know about the Japanese language, though. I've read poetry from several countries in the original, and my impression is that Japanese just can't break through the limitations of tanka and haiku. I mean, if you want to evoke the inner movements of the soul, all you get in modern Japanese is some sort of flat 'free verse.' Not that antique locutions like 'His Majesty's humble shield' (*shiko no mitate*) or 'Wondrous to tell' (*narinikeru kamo*) don't have their own kind of quaint appeal. That's why for the time being I don't plan to write any poetry in Japanese. I want to write novels. My idea is to achieve what you might call an impossible genre: the musical novel."

"That's a bit too difficult for me," she remarked.

At the top of the slope we came to Chieko's apartment building. There was no one else in the street. Silence reigned. Through the leaves clustered above us against the night sky you could see the light in her second-floor room. I stopped.

"I'll be going then," I said.

"Oh no, you have to take me *all* the way home."

"Why? Isn't this far enough?"

"I'm afraid I'll catch it from my mother if I let you leave me here. You don't mind, do you? It's only a little way."

I stood there, not knowing quite what to do. Chieko was gazing up at me, the picture of innocence. I took both her hands in mine, as though to warm them.

"The concert tonight was lovely, wasn't it?" I said.

"Mm." Chieko nodded. Then she exclaimed fervently, "Today was lovely! I'll never forget today!"

"Because the Chopin was so good?"

"No, because *we* were so good! The Chopin was just extra."

"What a sophist! And a while ago you were so impressed by Chopin!"

"Oh, I *was*!" She was in dead earnest. "Chopin was wonderful! That piano concerto is splendid. It's even more splendid, though, because we heard it together this evening."

"That's not really loving *music*."

"But it *is*! From now on, whenever I hear that piece, I'll remember that I heard it with *you*! For as long as I remember this evening, that music will be more dear, more incomparably precious to me than any other. Wouldn't that be loving music?"

I gently drew her hands toward me.

"May I?" I asked.

Chieko looked troubled, as though she were about to cry.

"Do we have to?" she said in a small, petulant voice.

"Not if you don't want to," I answered quickly, with a touch of annoyance.

With visible embarrassment Chieko tipped her head back and looked straight at me. Then, her small lips trembling slightly, she clumsily brought her face close to mine. I leaned down and touched my lips to hers. Cool, with at the same time the faint warmth of her breath . . . I had no chance to experience these, though. She brusquely withdrew her hands from mine and turned on her heel. "Bye-bye," she said and disappeared into the darkness, leaving me enveloped in a sweet scent.

You couldn't have called me a hard worker. Often enough I'd spread out a sheet of letter paper on my desk and, dictionary in hand, pointlessly look up the same word two or three times. Leaning on the windowsill, with the rapid clacking of typewriters behind me, I'd gaze at the grubby sky off toward the Shinagawa Fort. The office was on the fifth floor of a building near the Ginza. You could look straight down onto the streetcars, automobiles, and pedestrians, and count them like a procession of ants. On April eighteenth I was leaning on the windowsill when a lone American plane attacked Tokyo. That single, unfamiliar-looking gray aircraft made a strange sight as it came in at low altitude, almost grazing the roofs of the buildings off toward Tsukiji. The antiaircraft batteries sounded like exploding fireworks, and the puffs of smoke pursuing the plane resembled a row of Brussels sprouts. I shouted to my colleagues to come take a look, and we discussed whether it was really an enemy plane. Yes, the reality of war was coming closer, step by step. I had nothing to do that you could really call work, but I made myself look busy, and one by one I lined up on my desk all the volumes of an Italian encyclopedia. I'd hunt through them for the illustrations of Renaissance paintings, and while doing so I'd forget all my troubles. "Aha, studying, I see," the typist across from me would say with a smile, both hands flying. When the working day was over, those of us who got on well together would head for the München, nearby, and have a beer together. We were all miserable at heart, and sometimes intoxication only blackened our mood.

There was nothing back in my room to make me feel better. By the light of my familiar desk lamp I'd glance at the day's Petrarch sonnet, but the beautiful Laura had been gone for six hundred years, leaving behind only the poet's fleeting rhapsodies, set in futile type. I can't go on this way, I have to get down to my own work, I'd keep telling myself; but I also knew that, strive as I might, that red envelope would finish everything. Reading, writing—in the end, neither meant a thing. There I'd be, elbow on my desk and chin in hand, vacantly smoking a cigarette, when in the street outside a babble of voices, mingled with songs and *banzai* cries, would resound with indescribable sadness, all celebrating a new departure for the front. Never did I experience, as then, so overwhelming a longing to be with Chieko. All my anxiety would melt away if only I could hear her cheerful voice and hold her warm hand. Yet in the midst of my struggle against this fear that pervaded everything around me, like the air itself—this fear that the envelope might arrive at any moment—I stuck to my resolution not to seek refuge with her too easily. That didn't mean that I loved her any less. I could easily have gone to visit her every evening if I'd wished, and my feeling for her constantly urged me to do so. I derived a strange pleasure, though, from hardening my resistance to it. Nothing taught me the measure of my love for Chieko as thoroughly as these periods of separation, during which I repressed my feeling for her as much as I could. Love is endurance, a spiritual condition, an eternal present, a struggle against oblivion, while keeping company with the beloved, seeing her, talking with her, amount to mere phenomena. If Chieko and I truly loved each other, then our spirits should resonate together in their depths like two musical instruments and give off between them a subtle trill. So I believed, anyway. Despite my heartfelt love for her, I probably also made too much of my own solitude. Losing her brother had taught me all too well that in the end no flame of love, however intense, can melt the icy solitude into which we're born. Chieko was too young and innocent to see clearly into my wounded heart. I, on my side, meanwhile felt more alone the more I loved her, and I loved her more the more alone I felt. I could explain this psychological contradiction neither to myself nor to her.

"She's bound to be back by lunchtime," Chieko's mother assured me.

The warm, Sunday-morning sun shone uncomfortably on my back as I leaned against the window. With a show of hardly caring whether she was there or not, I smoked one cigarette after another. Just being in this room had a wonderfully soothing effect on me. Chieko's mother bustled about preparing lunch and so on, in her motherly way, and I could read or lounge about as I pleased. The Fujikis' place had long been where I felt most at home. In my undergraduate days I went there whenever I felt like it, and when the time came to eat, I'd perfectly naturally share their meal. I couldn't go there during the week any more after I got my job, but more often than not on Sundays I'd hang around all afternoon and have dinner with them. Even on my small salary I generally managed to bring something with me. Chieko's happy looks gave me a certain pride.

"You're so early today!" her mother remarked as she emerged from the kitchen. "We'll have lunch as soon as she gets back."

"I'm sorry for coming so soon. I got up much earlier than usual this morning."

"Oh, it's quite all right, Mr. Shiomi! You're welcome anytime! Oh, and Chieko was just delighted the other evening."

"The concert, you mean?"

"I heard the pianist was wonderful. She used to pester me about wanting to take piano lessons, you know."

"Can she play?"

"In the end I'm afraid she never took any lessons. We just couldn't afford it. I still regret that, though. It was all I could do, you see, just to keep two children in school."

"So Chieko's a neglected genius, for all we know?"

"Oh, hardly! It wouldn't have done her much good to become some sort of half-baked pianist. She's quite ordinary, unlike Shinobu. All she has to do is to graduate more or less respectably and then get married like any normal girl."

"Is she really that ordinary?"

"Does she strike *you* as a genius?"

I laughed. Deep down, though, all this left me with a slightly bitter aftertaste. Would Chieko's mother really let her daughter marry someone like me, an aspiring writer? I'd been assuming that marriage was something to be decided entirely between Chieko and me, but now, all of a sudden, her mother's comments sounded like a sort of roundabout refusal.

"Are you planning to find her a husband?" I asked on an impulse.

I knew as the words left my mouth that I shouldn't have spoken them, and I blushed; but she just smiled. "Would *you* be kind enough to marry her?" she asked in a perfectly normal tone.

Looking back, it seems to me that that moment was decisive. My life and Chieko's might have gone quite differently if I'd given her a straight answer. However, I couldn't get out anything better than a vaguely mumbled reply. Chieko's mother left it at that and moved on to another subject.

"She's due to graduate next year, you see," she said. "Considering that she's my only daughter, I'd really like to adopt a husband for her into the family, but I'm afraid we just don't have the means for that. So I suppose I might as well marry her off if anyone suitable turns up."

From there she went on to tell me about a relative of hers, a girl, who'd married recently.

We heard Chieko announce her return out at the entrance, and if I didn't follow her mother to the door, it's probably because of distress, somewhere deep within me, at being so unable to follow my heart. Chieko didn't appear, though, and I, too, went to the door, my hands in my pockets, when I heard a man's low voice mixed in among the conversation.

"What's going on, Chieko?" I asked.

"Oh, there you are! Mr. Yashiro says he won't come in."

"What? Yashiro? It's been a long time! How are you?"

"I'm sorry I haven't been in touch." There was a hint of formality in his voice.

"Come on in!"

"Do please come in!" Chieko's mother and I spoke together.

"No, I'm afraid I must be going. I have things to do. I promise to come again, though."

Yashiro gave me a smile, then said good-bye and turned to go.

"What a peculiar fellow!" Chieko muttered to herself as she took off her shoes.

"I wonder whether he left because I was here," I said.

"He's always so terribly reserved. He told me he'd see me home, but quite likely he never had any intention of actually coming in. It's a bit much, though. I can do without people like that."

"He *is* a pretty cold fish."

Chieko's critical remarks about Yashiro somehow bothered me, though. Back in those days he'd been her brother's closest friend. My heart would beat strangely whenever I saw the two of them caught up in conversation together, and, for me, love would suddenly turn then from a dreamed spiritual condition into the pain of life itself. Even now, amid a disquiet too slight to call jealousy, an odd impression of misalignment came over me like a premonition, as though all my love for Chieko were a misapprehension and life were going on somewhere apart from my real growth.

During the meal we found ourselves talking about Fujiki's friends back then among his classmates. All were now employed and many, like Mori, had gone into the military. Yashiro worked in a big electrical goods factory, while Ishii had stayed on at his university as an assistant in the physics department. Both regularly attended Reverend Sawada's Bible-study meetings, and Chieko, who saw a lot of them, knew a good deal about how they were getting on. I sometimes wondered, though, during all this talk of one old acquaintance or another, what the late Fujiki Shinobu would have been up to if he had lived, and I kept a discreet eye on his mother's face. She looked as cheerful as ever, and eating with the family this way gave me the illusion that I was suddenly Fujiki himself.

While relaxing after lunch I casually asked Chieko, "How serious *is* Yashiro, anyway?"

"About what?"

"About Sawada's Bible-study meetings. Why is everyone going to them? Isn't it a bit of a fad?"

"You're awful! Yashiro and Ishii are both perfectly serious. To me their faith seems entirely genuine."

"This Sawada must be a good man. Even *I* have read his stuff, and I'm impressed. He's great. Still, if it's his personal attraction people go to the meetings for, then what they get there must be more his personal Christianity than the real thing. That's what I imagine, anyway."

"There isn't any 'real Christianity,'" Chieko replied heatedly. "I suppose it's real enough when an ordained minister speaks Christian truths as a representative of his faith. But real Christianity is written in the Bible, though—all you have to do is read it. So anyone who wants to repent of his sins and lead a new life under the guidance of the risen Christ can become a real Christian. There's no need for baptism or the sacraments. Listening to Sawada's lectures on the Bible just confirms us in our own, inner faith."

"It still sounds to me like proselytizing for Non-Church Christianity," I said. "Sawada's gatherings aren't church services, are they?"

"No, they're not. I'm no expert on the subject, but Jesus never founded a church in his lifetime. Paul's the one who did that. I expect he had to, after Jesus died, so as to propagate Christianity in opposition to Judaism. Even then, though, the church at Corinth was degenerate enough to arouse Paul's wrath. Living spiritual vigor naturally declines when it becomes formalized. Not even the congregations that Luther and Calvin founded in opposition to the Catholic Church could fully recapture the spirit of Paul. That's because the whole notion of a church was wrong from the start. Jesus never said a word to suggest that you have to go to church to be saved. He did say, though, 'Wherever two or three of you gather in my name, I will be among you. What he meant was that any repentant sinner is a member of the Church of Christ, and that those who share their faith naturally share their love as well. Our gatherings at Professor Sawada's have a different meaning than ordinary church services."

"I see. You're so eloquent, Chieko."

"I hate the way you make fun of me," she retorted angrily.

I smoked my cigarette and studied her earnest expression. Her mother had finished tidying up and was now reading the newspaper next to her. Mild afternoon sunlight shone in through the window.

"In middle school I used to attend services at a Protestant church, you know," I began quietly, in a reminiscing mood. "I read the Bible a lot. I didn't really understand it, but I do think I read it seriously. And I went to church. I never could feel at home in the church atmosphere, though. I felt as though my idea of Christianity, and the Christianity I found in church, were different. In Bible class I noticed that the students were all just doing supplementary study for their exams, and I couldn't make anything of the gatherings of the congregation, except that the members seemed just to have chosen the church for their social get-togethers. The pastor wasn't financially independent, and he did whatever the foreign mission society said. I didn't like the way he cared only about keeping up the number of active mem-

bers and ingratiated himself with everyone to collect more dona-
tions. I suppose the worst was his sermons, though. Pedestrian
interpretations, lukewarm platitudes—they offered no inspiration whatever. All they did for me was dilute the seriousness of
my interest. It's just another job, isn't it, I'd say to myself, and I'm
sorry to say that I spent my time during the sermons finding fault
with them. I became completely disillusioned, and in the end I
never went back."

"So, you see, Non-Church Christianity is the only answer,"
Chieko broke in enthusiastically.

"Perhaps you're right. That's how I felt, anyway, at least back
then. I read the Bible, put my faith in Jesus, and wanted to act according to his word. I thought it'd be enough if I upheld the Bible
and sought salvation from Christ in full awareness of my sins. I
didn't see the slightest need to go to church."

"So, for you, all you needed was yourself."

"That's right. If I believe in God from the bottom of my heart,
then *that's* real Non-Church Christianity, isn't it?"

"I'd say it's more like pride," Chieko replied quietly.

That stung me, and I retorted vehemently.

"To you it probably sounds like pride because I'm the one who
said it. I prefer to keep the question on a general level. Say someone reads the Bible alone, believes it, repents his sins, puts his faith
in Jesus, and so resolves to lead a new life. Having no one to share
his faith with, he prays and believes alone. Is that person then not
a Christian?"

"I'm not sure, but I do know that the Church doesn't yet recognize as a Christian someone who hasn't been baptized. That

seems right to us. Not even the Non-Church movement necessarily considers baptism trivial or meaningless. I do think faith alone is enough, though, even without baptism. But there's just one thing . . ."

"What?"

Chieko frowned a little and looked down at her hands. Then in a moment she looked up again. Her eyes were clear and beautiful.

"Well, to me, you see, faith is joy. Hearing the Gospel makes you so happy you want to tell other people about it. When the joy of faith fills your heart you can't bear to keep it to yourself, you want desperately to pass it on—it's something like that. So it seems to me quite natural that there should emerge a genuinely spiritual fellowship of people in loving communion with one another—a fellowship quite different from the churches of the past, formalized, traditional, and set in their ways as they are. I just can't imagine that kind of isolated, wholly individual faith."

"Really? It says in the Bible that the poor in spirit will attain the kingdom of heaven. I don't quite understand who the poor in spirit *are*, but Jesus certainly called out repeatedly to the wretched, the heavily burdened, the meek. So is it really impossible for someone like that, someone truly humble, to read the Bible reverently, believe in God, and quietly keep that faith to himself, in his heart? Someone, let's say, who's so poor in spirit that his faith never turns to visible joy and remains hidden within him all his life? Is faith like that, wholly individual faith, really a sin?"

"I don't know," Chieko answered.

"For example, one of the things I didn't understand back then is the parable of the talents. Could I have a look at your Bible?"

On returning from Sawada's meeting Chieko had just dropped her bag on her desk. She now took a small Bible from it and gave it to me. I leafed through its pages.

"It's in Matthew. Ah, I've got it. A man setting out on a journey calls his three servants together and entrusts each of them, according to his ability, with five silver talents, two silver talents, and just one. While he's away the servant with the five talents invests them and turns them into ten, and the one with two talents similarly doubles his. Their master praises the two, calling them good and faithful. The one who got just one talent, though—he comes to his master and says, 'Lord, I knew thee that thou art an hard man, reaping where thou hast not sown, and gathering where thou hast not strawed: And I was afraid, and went and hid thy talent in the earth: lo, there thou hast that is thine.' And this is what his master answers: 'Thou wicked and slothful servant, thou knewest that I reap where I sowed not, and gather where I have not strawed: Thou oughtest therefore to have put my money to the exchangers, and then at my coming I should have received mine own with usury. Take therefore the talent from him, and give it unto him which hath ten talents. For unto everyone that hath shall be given, and he shall have abundance; but from him that hath not shall be taken away even that which he hath. And cast ye the unprofitable servant into outer darkness: there shall be weeping and gnashing of teeth.'"

"That has something to do with the kingdom of heaven, doesn't it?" Chieko put in.

"It seems to. Just before that, it says you have to keep your eyes open to enter the kingdom of heaven. So this business of having to double your five talents, if you have them, means you're duty-bound to pass the Gospel on others once you've heard it. In fact, as I understand it, it's your duty to bring in new believers. Isn't that a bit much?"

"Umm . . ."

"Come to think of it, this master knew perfectly well from the start that the servant he'd given just one talent was the least capable of the three, since he gave his servants the talents according to their ability. This one was a timid, pusillanimous fellow, and he was afraid of losing what he'd been so solemnly given, so he carefully buried it somewhere. He didn't waste his silver, and he didn't run off with it. Nonetheless, his master banished him into the outer darkness. Was what he did really such a crime?"

"I don't know."

"No doubt God *is* a harsh master. He's *too* harsh. And maybe this thing called religion is just the same. You amass what capital you can, you recruit just one new believer if that's the best you can do, and if you don't, the whole thing falls down. In that sense it's all very businesslike, which I suppose is natural enough. I had my doubts, though, back then. The servant with five talents did very well by making more, but he'd have been thrown out if instead he'd lost some. You might say he was saddled from the start with the obligation to make more."

"Believing, though, means being responsible for your faith, doesn't it?"

"Probably. But I just don't understand the master's reason for banishing the servant who'd buried his one talent in the ground. He wasn't smart or resourceful, he just dumbly followed his master's orders. Wouldn't it be fair to say that if that's enough to get him banished, then the religion involved is just too strict, or inhuman, or profit-minded?"

Chieko sighed. "This is a hard one. I'll think about it some more. But, Shiomi-san, are you really talking about yourself?"

I put down my cigarette, sipped some tea, and wondered why we'd ever started this discussion. Still, I couldn't avoid answering her.

"I once had a solitary faith of my own," I began slowly. "But then they told me that that wasn't faith at all, and that solitude and faith couldn't coexist. My kind of Christianity was even more Non-Church than yours—I suppose it was less religion than a kind of ethical stance. I agreed with the way Jesus had lived and with what he'd taught. But despite being unbearably alone, I still couldn't give up my solitude in order to cling to God. The parable of the talents isn't the only thing that tripped me up. We humans are weak, and things trip us up all the time. When I tripped, though, I wanted the responsibility to be mine. I chose my own solitude over God. The outer darkness seemed a more human place to be."

"But isn't it being alone that makes us seek God in the first place?"

"Usually, I suppose. No doubt solitude is weak, and shows how powerless and miserable we all are. It was strong for *me*, though— it was the last bastion that sustained me. That was pride, I suppose. Still, I felt that a man's weakness is his own responsibility, and I didn't want to sell out my freedom to the point of bowing before God. When your brother died I rejected God, the Buddha, everything. I bitterly regretted ever having felt anything for so pitiless a deity. I'll never forget that feeling."

I looked down, said no more, and lit a cigarette. Chieko and her mother remained silent as well.

"It seems to me that killing God made me stronger. Of course, even now I believe in Jesus's moral teaching. And I feel acutely what he must have felt as he wandered the desolate lake and plains of Galilee, or suffered in Gethsemane, when he said his soul was 'exceeding sorrowful, even unto death.' But all that probably just comes down to my literary sentimentality. Presumably it has little to do with *your* faith, or the faith of your friends."

"Shiomi-san," Chieko said sadly, "I don't believe the flame of your faith is completely extinguished yet."

"I talk too much," I replied.

"I'll think about all this. You won't be angry, will you?"

"About what?" I exhaled smoke toward the ceiling and leaned back with one elbow on the tatami.

"As I understand it you once had faith, all by yourself. You told no one else about it, and you never shared the joy of it with anyone else. Mightn't *that* be the reason your faith left you? Mightn't it mean that the solitary faith we were talking about isn't enough?"

"You mean that I wouldn't have lost my faith if only I'd submitted to the strictures of form, had myself baptized, and gone regularly to church? Real faith surely has nothing to do with going regularly to church, or with allowing yourself or not to be spurred on to greater faith by your friends. I suppose that from *your* point of view I lost my faith because the Holy Spirit abandoned me, or because some demon led me astray, or something like that. Myself, though, I'd say that *I* abandoned God. My will to get stronger made me do it. No, I'm not the one who lost out."

"I'm so sorry," she whispered.

"There's nothing to be sorry about," I said.

"And you're not lonely?"

"Of course I'm lonely. But I don't mind."

I stood up, went to the wide-open window, and looked down. Green trees lined both sides of the street as it wound its way down to the foot of the hill, where the railroad right-of-way, with all its many tracks, cut across it. Beyond the tracks stretched the grubby roofs of the shopping district, factory chimneys belching smoke, and in the distance the misty gray sea. My mind felt as dingy as the view.

What could have caused this sudden surge of self-hatred, this peculiar sadness, this wretched feeling of being lonely and lost? If Chieko, the Chieko I loved, saw the world completely differently from me, then there was little chance that we could really love each other. However much I might love her, she could hardly love *me*—the me who'd chosen solitude to strengthen his prideful self. Perhaps that me had been looking for a little love from Chieko. Where love is concerned, simply loving should be enough.

"Shiomi-san!" Chieko called from behind me. "Won't you come with me to one of Reverend Sawada's meetings?"

I turned to face her. "Why?" I asked, and sat down on the balcony.

"I think someone like you could become a truly marvelous Christian. I think you could attain a depth of faith far beyond mine. As Reverend Sawada once said, the most hopeless people of all are the ones who just don't care. Agnostics, he said, and people who've stumbled and suffered many times, they're the ones who can become true Christians. So . . ."

"But it wouldn't make any difference," I murmured, glancing obliquely at her fervent face. "Just going along with someone else, without any heartfelt purpose of my own—no, that wouldn't help at all. It'd be a lot better for your mother to go with you."

"Who, me?" said her mother. "This discussion of yours has been so difficult, I've paid no attention to it."

Smiling, she looked from the magazine she'd been reading. Chieko caught her smile.

"Mother always says she doesn't want to go."

"Well, at my age you don't feel like getting around that much."

"Really? Just mention going to the theater and you're off like a shot."

Mother and daughter laughed pleasantly together, but my heart remained shrouded in gloom. The buzzing of a tiny airplane, high up in the sky, resonated painfully within the vast loneliness of a heart constantly pricked by anxiety. I just couldn't go on this way, time for me was chopped into bits, there was no peace for me anywhere . . .

"I'll be going," I said.

Chieko's glance was both surprised and accusing. Despite the smile still on her lips, her eyes looked like those of a tearful child. Her mother joined her in urging me to stay.

"There's still something I have to do today."

"Why, you're as bad as Mr. Yashiro!"

"It's true, I really do!" I, too, was smiling.

As I moved to get up, I suddenly remembered.

"Ah, yes, where did I put it? Mrs. Fujiki, I did leave a packet wrapped in paper somewhere, didn't I?"

"Yes, I'll get it."

She brought the packet in from the next room. "It's for Chieko," I said, stepping out into the entrance. I bent down to put on my shoes.

"What's is it?" Chieko inquired.

"Open it later. You'll see."

"Why, it can't be that much of a mystery! May I open it now?"

"Of course."

Off came the wrapping. "Oh my goodness!" she cried.

The packet contained three large-format volumes of sheet music. She inspected the title on each.

"'Piano Concerto No. 1'—that's the piece we heard, isn't it. Then this one is a collection of waltzes, and this one a collection of ballades. What's all this about?"

"They're for you."

"Really? Why, how absolutely *lovely*!" she exclaimed, dancing for joy like a child. "I'm so happy! Look, Mother, look what Shiomi-san has given me!"

Her mother joined her, wreathed in smiles. With my hand on the front door I added, "You said you loved Chopin, so I hunted them up for you. It's very hard these days to find imported music."

"This is *so* kind of you!" she kept saying gaily as she turned the pages. To me, the musical notation looked like some sort of dubious cipher.

"Good-bye, then."

I went out the door. "Wait!" I heard Chieko calling behind me as I hurried down the stairs. I followed the road for a while, somewhat hesitantly at first because I thought she might come after me, but then resolutely quickening my pace. The air was warm, and at that speed I soon broke out in a sweat, but I forged straight ahead as though fleeing a pursuer. Even while striding along like that, though, and then riding in the train, I couldn't repress the feeling that, just as everything around me was sliding backwards and out of sight, something, too, was slipping away from my heart.

I began writing my novel.

I was alone. At work every day I hardly spoke to anyone except about office matters, and when the time came I'd go straight home and shut myself up in my room. There, by lamplight, I kept writing away, constantly aware that my purpose in doing so was to reinforce my solitude.

It was an odd novel, the one I was writing. I can't even remember it very well any more. It was set in a time neither present nor past, but somehow transparent, and in a place that was neither here nor there, but like somewhere remembered in a dream. The characters were a nameless youth and a nameless girl. Sometimes they went traveling together, sometimes they separated and across great distances thought fondly of each other. It had neither plot nor story, and everything in it merged together as in a dream. The form resembled that of a sonata: a first theme (solitude) and a second theme (love) recurred, unfolded, and reached a conclusion. No, actually, there was no conclusion. My violins just repeated themselves ad infinitum. Amid all this I led a sort of separate life of my own.

I never went back to see Chieko. In the midst of my solitude I experienced a sense of guilt. I'd been unusually sensitive since childhood to the prick of conscience. The odor of sin clung to everything I did. Even when I was in love—yes, even when I loved Fujiki Shinobu—this horrible notion constantly caused me deep torment. I also felt unbearably depraved when there sometimes drifted over my feeling for Chieko, like a cloud, an awareness of her as a woman. (Things were different when it came to fiction, though. I can't explain this strange contradiction. For example, I gladly praised such novels as Huysmans's *À rebours* and *Là-Bas*. I also was mad about the religious paintings of Pietro Perugino, an unsavory character entirely without faith in God. Nonetheless, I had no sense of being somehow a divided personality.)

Like a hunted beast I licked my wounds and kept running. Sometimes it still occurred to me to wonder whether I was really guilty of any crime and whether this invisible evil pursuing me, this actual evil settling over me like a canopy, wasn't too immeasurably vast. My wish to nurse my solitude, my insistence on strengthening it by fighting the honeyed seductions of the desire to see Chieko, probably had nothing to do with licking my wounds and writing my novel. Still, my heart enjoyed no freedom apart simply from writing my novel and irresistibly loving her.

I feared the war. It's not that I entertained some theoretical notion that it represented absolute evil. No, the feeling was more personal than that. It was a powerful fear that merged with my natural cowardice into an almost physical terror. I instinctively hated war—any war that deserved the name. I'd grown up in the waning years of the left-wing movement, and my environment had never encouraged me to study Marxism, but I certainly would have had far more sympathy for those people's views if they hadn't looked forward to a final, bloody revolution. In a word, I was against everything—Christianity, Marxism, the family, school—but my opposition was never more than lukewarm, and it never inconvenienced me. I couldn't manage to make myself a dilettante, an academic, or a writer. I was just a dithering, lost, fearful, lonely youth. Ever since middle school, however, I'd been sharply opposed to the growing trend toward militarism. I avoided military training as much as possible, and I got all the way through college without ever learning to break down a rifle. Of course, I knew perfectly well that such negative resistance amounted to nothing. During the three months leading up to my draft fitness exam I ate nothing but udon noodles and water, lost all the weight I possibly could, and showed up for the exam hardly more than skin and bone. To my surprise, though, I got only a second-class classification for it. My hero was a friend who'd successfully had himself classified third-class by drinking two quarts of soy sauce on the morning of his exam. But every one of us was still in immediate danger of being drafted as a reservist. Some were sensitive to this danger, others less so, but nobody was more acutely aware of it than me.

No doubt the first fear war inspired in me was for my life itself—a primitive, instinctive fear of the annihilation of self. This fear then merged with another, just as strong: that of killing another human being. I'd never had the slightest desire to kill anyone. In the end, would I really be capable of killing, if cornered into doing so by my superiors, or, if it came down to killing or being killed, in the name of legitimate self-defense? I shrank from the thought of dying myself, but those terrifying words "kill a person" were more than enough to unnerve my conscience. Besides, the enemy in question—what was he, after all? He wasn't *my* enemy. Why should people have to kill each other over some stupid difference of ideology? My chosen field of study had been comparative linguistics and literature, so I suppose my thinking had been nurtured naturally enough by the Greek ideal of *kosmopolitês*. However, everything I felt as a citizen of the world conflicted with what I was required to feel as a Japanese. Now that the war was under way, the more heavily the danger of being drafted at any moment weighed on me, like a miasma, the more all my thoughts turned helplessly to a single issue: how to bring myself to take up arms. Constantly I asked myself, "Can you kill? Will you die?"

Meanwhile, every evening I continued writing my novel—that dreamlike novel, utterly unrelated to reality. Yes, unrelated; yet in this dreamy atmosphere my hero still experienced pure anguish, and to that extent my work was perhaps not yet truly escapist—or, at least, the time I spent at it could still be counted as a genuine part of my life. (To me, right now, life is writing this memoir.)

When the weight of immediate reality bit too cruelly into my shoulders, however, the image of myself on the battlefield, a marionette without personal will, haunted me like a hallucination. I put down my pen, stared blankly at the words I'd just begun writing, then abruptly shoved on my geta and went outside. What future did my novel have? No one would read it. No one would understand it. What good could it possibly do me, when I went off to the front, to have covered all that paper with writing? There in a dim, otherwise deserted coffee shop, I propped my elbows on a table, a beer before me, and endlessly repeated to myself the same, unanswerable questions.

The sleepy-looking waitress sat down across from me.

"You want another? Just for you."

"Sure."

I drank the insipid beer and watched her feeding herself peanuts.

"Are you a poet?" she suddenly asked.

"What a question! Why do you ask?"

"It just struck me that you might be. Are you?"

"I suppose so."

"How nice! I read a poem a while ago. It was great. 'The Song of the Southward Advance,' it was called."

I laughed. So this was the masterpiece of the man reputed to be Japan's greatest poet! The Muse would weep.

"Why not show me your poetry, next time?"

A sleepy, stupid face, hands mechanically shucking peanuts, and there, across from her, dejectedly drinking his lonely beer, me.

"What time is it?" I asked.

"About seven, I think. We're open till nine—there's no rush."

Nonetheless I got up in silence, paid my bill, and left.

When I got back, my plump landlady informed me at the entrance that I had a visitor. "It's a woman," she added with a bright smile before I could ask her more, "a young lady." I hurried down the corridor to my room, muttering to myself on the way, "Well, this *is* a surprise! Who can it be?"

There, sitting at my desk, her back to me against the light of the lamp, was Chieko.

"Chieko! What's happened?"

"Where *were* you, Shiomi-san? I got nervous, waiting here like this—I was thinking of leaving."

"I just went out for a walk." I went over and stood beside her. "That's my only chair you're sitting on. How about the tatami?"

Chieko sniffed the air around my face like a puppy. "Oh dear," she said, "you've been drinking again."

"Only a little, really." Chieko turned fully toward me, her legs dangling from the chair. I put my hands on her shoulders and brought my face closer to hers.

"All right?"

"No!" she exclaimed loudly and announced, "I can't stand people who drink!"

"I've put you off," I said with a smile and sat down cross-legged on the tatami at her feet.

"Shiomi-san, why haven't you come around in all this time?"

"I've been busy."

"Oh? Anyway, thank you so much!"

"For what?"

"For Chopin! Why, you forget everything! The waltzes are really lovely. It'll be so nice if I ever get to be able to play them."

"But what brings you here this evening, so late? It's the first time you've ever been to my place, isn't it?"

"Yes, it is. Mother might well give me a piece of her mind if she knew."

She shrugged her shoulders and gave me a sly grin. She waggled her legs around on the chair.

"You see," she began, "today Reverend Sawada gave a public lecture at the university. I went with a classmate friend, and I have to be back at Ochanomizu Station by eight."

"I see. So there's still time."

"About half an hour." She checked her watch as she spoke.

"Shall I go and get some tea?"

"Oh no, don't bother. Why haven't you been over, though? Is it because I suggested you come to one of our meetings?"

"No, of course not. I've just been busy, as I told you."

"Doing what? Something for your job?"

"No, writing my novel."

"Ah, yes, that's what I thought, with all these sheets of manu-script paper on your desk. Are you getting it done?"

"No, I'm afraid, not yet. I'm not getting anywhere. And I have a lot of things on my mind."

"Like what?"

She dropped her gaze to look gravely down on me from above. The lamp set one side of her face dazzlingly aglow, and stray locks of her hair glittered in the light.

"Umm, I'm not sure how to explain it." Looking down in some embarrassment, I found my eyes resting on Chieko's knees. Their slim, sock-clad lines were jiggling a little.

"In a word, it's the war. I know I'll be drafted soon. I'm sure you can understand the dread I feel."

"Oh, I do," she answered earnestly. "Even *we* will most likely be drafted for labor duty when we graduate. And if we get married then, we'll have to wait on our own till our husbands return." She spoke this last sentence at breakneck speed.

"It's a lot worse, though, for those of us who really are called up to fight. And why should we have to go? They're lucky, those who can gladly answer, 'Banzai! Selfless sacrifice! A holy war!' and so on, and really believe what they're saying. For myself, I accept none of it. No doubt Japan has a domineering America pressing it hard and may lose its supply routes, but Japan is also clearly imperialist in Manchuria and China. Anyway, what in the world makes it so important to link up with barbarian countries like Italy and Germany to wage such a reckless war? Maybe Japan *will* win. Things are going well at the moment. But what will we get out of killing tens of thousands, no, hundreds of thousands of people? What good will glory that empty do us?"

Chieko said nothing. I pressed her knees together between my hands.

"War means treating human lives like dirt. Take me, for instance. In no time war will sweep away everything I am—my loves, my sorrows, my joys, the little talent I have. Illness is what caused your brother's death, and even then I couldn't accept it. It was God's will—if you accept that there *is* a God. But war's a matter of human will. America's no more an enemy than Japan is a friend. It's the warmongers in America and the warmongers in Japan who thirst for blood and killing. And we're the ones who get killed. So tens of thousands of young men, talented young men like your brother, get themselves killed as simple soldiers. Why, oh why should we all go off to die?"

Chieko made no reply. She murmured, "You might *not* die, though." Then she added, even lower, "I don't *want* you to die!"

I pressed her warm legs harder between my palms. I was too wrought up now to stop the flow of words.

"It's not so much dying I'm afraid of," I said. "Naturally everyone's afraid of that. It's not just that *I'll* die, though, if I go off to war; it's that I'm all too likely to kill somebody else. Modern warfare seldom involves hand-to-hand, face-to-face combat, but even so, the bullet

I fire may well directly kill another young man just like me. No one can be sure it won't. So for fear of committing murder I won't actually be able to fire properly at all, unless I fire into the air. Is that being a coward? Or is it just being sentimental? I talked to some friends about this, and all they did was laugh. They told me I'd soon get used to it, we're all the product of our environment, and there's no point in fretting like that ahead of time. I wonder, though. What could be more terrifying than the idea of just getting used to it? Every shred of spiritual freedom would be gone then. Is the sole purpose of war to inure people to massacring one another? If it is, then why do we have to sacrifice ourselves to the despicable folly of war?"

Chieko began to say something but stopped. Hugging her knees harder than ever, I kept talking.

"I don't believe in God any more, but I still know with every fiber of my being that killing is evil. I don't care whether or not my soul is saved. *Post mortem nihil est*. But can a Christian who kills the enemy in war really go to heaven? Or is all that insignificant in the face of a greater necessity? That's my question to the Christians."

"I don't know," Chieko murmured.

"So could *you* kill an enemy, if you were ordered to?"

"No, I couldn't," she answered, a little louder.

"That's what you'd be forced into doing, though, if you were in my shoes. If I fire my rifle into the air, then it'll be my turn to be killed. So when it comes right down to it, I can't be sure what I'll actually do. I can't guarantee that I won't kill, and I hate that. Everything seems to go dark before my eyes when I think about it."

I was breathing hard, still clutching Chieko's knees. Her hands gently stroked my head.

"I came to reject Christianity even more after this war started, and you know why? Because Christians accepted the war without a qualm. Why don't they oppose it? Why don't they try to stop it? This attack on Pearl Harbor came before we even knew it. No one did anything whatsoever to prevent it—oh no! American Christians pray for the victory of God and democracy, British Christians do the same for the victory of God and king, and Japanese Christians pray for the victory of God and emperor. What God are they praying to, I'd like to know? Japan, for its part, has committed all sorts of atrocities in China, there's no doubt about that. But the Christians did nothing to oppose that war, did they! And now we're stuck with this one, too. So are the souls of Christians really going to be saved?"

"We're suffering too, you know," Chieko said.

Through the window came, in a sadly resonant chorus, voices singing an army song to celebrate a new departure for the front. I looked up. Chieko's face loomed above me.

"There they go again," I went on. "Draftees have been out there practically every evening lately. I just don't know what to do with myself when I hear those songs. They know nothing, any of them, and they've been told nothing. Off they go, all lying to themselves, with their happy faces and their *banzai* for the 'Great Japanese Empire,' for 'His Majesty the Emperor.' They're so stupid, so utterly stupid!"

Chieko, still looking down at me, had one hand around my neck to draw my head toward her, and with the other she was stroking my hair. The hand on my hair trembled a little. The trembling increased with each distant roar of "Banzai! Banzai!" I buried my face in her lap.

I was happy that way. With my hands around her knees, my face in her lap, and her hand stroking my hair, my violent agitation subsided, leaving behind it only a pure, cleansed happiness. This, too, is something life has to offer, I thought to myself; and no doubt it's also just part of life miserably to risk your physical and spiritual freedom at the boundary between life and death. So why, why can't this moment, this high tide moment of shared love, go on forever? Is this real and the other false? Is the other real and *this* false—this moment like a sweet-smelling flower? Why doesn't *this* stand as happy proof of being alive?

I lifted my head. Chieko's shining eyes came very close, tender and solicitous. Her face, unmoving as a sculpture, merged for me with that of the heroine in the novel I was writing. Time stopped.

It was Chieko who drew my face toward hers. Her cool, fragrant lips settled on mine, sweeping me beyond forgetting and delight. Pristine, yet rich with every passion, they created between heaven and earth a lasting, breathless silence.

Only for an instant, though. Abruptly she withdrew her face, turned away toward my desk, and buried her face in her hands. I rested my head again on her lap.

"'The girl awaited eternity. When night, like a colossal hand governing the constellations, slowly relinquishes the vastness of its dominion, and in the orient sky the barest glimmer of dawn begins to extinguish the sleeping stars . . .'"

It was from the manuscript that I'd left lying on my desk. Chieko had apparently begun reading it aloud, very low.

"'. . . when the bird upon the bough wakens early to first light, the babbling brook hastens its flow toward the beckoning sea, and meadow grasses bow lower still beneath their burden of dew;

when golden arrows pierce the zenith, the knowing cock nobly crows his harbinger of morning, and the mystery of night gives way at last to the plain truth of day—who then could deny the touch of eternity? The girl pursed her lips and gazed afar in anticipation of this eternity. The great change—smooth, intricate, swift—went forward apace, yet in its very midst the flow for an instant paused, and the spell so long awaited answered her yearning, as though descending upon her from heaven.'"

My draft stopped there. In the ensuing silence the entire work surged into my mind, clear, like a revelation, and, together with my present happiness, inspiration flooded through me like a tide. I *will* write this novel! I'm going to *live* it! Oh, Chieko, Chieko, just as long as you'll live with me . . .!

"I'd better be going," she said.

I looked up, as though waking from a dream. "Ouch!" she cried—I must have squeezed her knees too tightly.

"Sorry, I was daydreaming. Isn't it too late?"

"It's after eight o'clock, but that's still all right."

I quickly got to my feet. Chieko stood up from the chair, took my hand, and smiled in a manner quite different from before.

"My friend Suga will have left by now. I'm sure she's angry," she said. Then she squeezed my hand. "Will you see me off as far as Ochanomizu Station?"

"Of course I will."

We decided to walk and plunged side by side into the press of people along Hongō Avenue. The crowds thinned out once we passed the 3-chōme intersection. Now and again a brightly lit streetcar went by along the darkened avenue. Shoulder to shoulder we walked, close, each step resonating around us. I couldn't tell what Chieko was thinking because she remained silent and kept her gaze fixed straight ahead. Foolishly enough, I assumed that she was listening to the fading echoes of the same joy I had felt. *She* had kissed *me* just a little while ago. The music of intoxication still resounded in my ears.

"Are you going somewhere for the summer vacation, Chieko?" I asked. "To your uncle's place, perhaps?"

This was where her brother had died. Chieko nodded vaguely.

"And I may go to Lake Yamanaka, too."

"For fun?"

"Reverend Sawada's Bible study group meets there every year. I may join them."

"You're not going to Oiwake? Your school has a lodge there, doesn't it?"

"Yes, it does. Come to think of it, we're all graduating next year, so I might go with my friends, if *they* go. Why do you ask?"

"Well, the people where I work all take a week's summer vacation, in turns. I've been planning mine for perhaps in late August, and on a friend's recommendation I've been thinking of spending it at an inn in Oiwake. If you'll be there at your school lodge, we'll be able to walk together in the mountains."

"That's right, we will." She nodded again.

Her answer lacked any spark of enthusiasm. There was something dull and mechanical about it. We reached the station and looked around the brightly lit ticket gate, but no one hailed us. It was now after eight thirty.

"Sure enough, she's left ahead of me. How about going out on the bridge there and talking a little more?"

I was glad to retrace our steps a bit. We leaned on the railing and peered down toward the dark waters of the moat. Off to one side, the sparsely frequented station platform glowed dimly. You could make out neither the color of the water nor the shape of the boats floating on it. All that rose from down there was a kind of sour smell.

"Shiomi-san . . ." Chieko addressed me with a touch of formality in her voice.

"What?" I answered cheerfully.

Beside me, she, too, was looking down toward the dark moat. After hesitating a moment she looked up at me. Her eyes were moist, as though she were crying.

"Shiomi-san," she said again.

"Well, what?"

"I think . . . I think perhaps we shouldn't see each other any more."

I almost jumped. I couldn't believe what I'd just heard.

"Let's not see each other any more. It'll be better that way."

"What is this, suddenly?"

"I've been thinking for quite a while. It's no good. We'd just be unhappy. You *do* see what I mean, don't you?"

"No, I don't. Absolutely not. Why should we be unhappy?"

Big tears fell from her eyes. I took her hand and drew her face close to mine.

"Why are you saying this?" I whispered in her ear.

Chieko, her lips trembling, made no reply. She was gazing down over the railing, looking indescribably lonely. Sick at heart, I had no idea what to say. I couldn't begin to imagine why she should have taken it into her head to talk such nonsense.

"Chieko," I began, shaking her a little.

"I'm sorry," she said. She sharply withdrew her hand from my grasp and, in the same instant, said, "Good-bye." Free now, she ran toward the station.

"Chieko! Chieko!" I shouted after her.

The shock was too sudden, though, and I remained rooted to the spot. Stop seeing each other, split up? Any number of explanations formed in my head, only to vanish like foam on a stream. Not one of them made sense. Hadn't she and I been happy together just now? We'd trusted each other, we'd understood each other, we'd loved each other—hadn't we?

Right under my eyes, a train heading in Chieko's direction came thundering into the station amid shooting sparks. Presumably she'd be boarding it to go home. The bell stopped ringing, the conductor gave his signal, and the train started moving again, picking up speed until it vanished into the distance. Why? I just stood there as though forgetting to move, gazing off toward where the train had disappeared. The water's somehow fishy, sinister smell rose to fill the silence around me.

My draft notice didn't come that summer. In late August I went to spend my summer vacation week at the village of Oiwake in Nagano Prefecture.

It was a poor little village of a few houses scattered, as though forgotten, along the old Shinano highway below Mount Asama. You got there from the Shin'etsu Line station after a stroll of hardly more than a mile through a larch wood. The view opened out after a barely noticeable bend in the path to reveal the mountain, a faint plume of smoke trailing from its summit, towering over the village roofs, the fire lookout tower, and the surrounding forest. The corn rose taller than a man, its ripe ears swaying in the early autumn wind, and the buckwheat fields were flowering white Rather grubby children ran merrily around on the dusty road. It was a peaceful, infinitely tranquil scene. The correspondingly rustic inn stood, all alone, beside the road.

Here, just a few hours from the office where I worked, with its big windows giving onto the Ginza crowds, the stillness seemed to flow through me like spring water. The mass of people in the city no doubt hardened my isolation, but amid this cleansed and carefree solitude I found myself powerless to resist. I merged with the landscape. A little way along the road I came to the fork where the old Hokkoku Road—the one they call Wakasare—and the Nakasendō Road meet. I sat down on a rock, gazed at the moss-covered stone Buddhas nearby, and vividly pictured the daimyo processions that must once have passed so colorfully by. Those walking this same Wakasare must have thought back longingly to the Edo they had left far behind. No doubt some sickened on their journey, or even died and left their bones buried by the roadside. Meanwhile time ran on, the smoke of Asama quietly rained ash on the surrounding villages, plants bloomed and scattered seed, and travelers felt in their hearts emotions as fleeting as the smoke.

There on the second floor of the inn, with the sound of the nearby stream in my ears, I felt a surge of melancholy. After sundown large moths and tiny flying ants invaded my room to get at the bare light bulb and went fluttering about everywhere. I spread my manuscript on the cheap desk and lost myself in thought—about what, I wonder? Probably about forgetting.

Fujiki Shinobu had died already several years ago. By slow degrees I'd begun to forget what he looked like, this friend I'd once loved so ardently. Can human passion really be *that* fleeting in the end, that selfish, that fickle? And Fujiki Chieko—I'd had no contact with her since our miserable parting that night at Ochanomizu Station. She'd forgotten me, and I her. To accept a new reality, must we always bury our old joys and sorrows somewhere out of mind? Can we really forget it all for the sake of new pain, new suffering?

Actually, I hadn't forgotten Chieko at all. On the contrary, my heart longed for her more than ever. Whenever I sat at my desk in the evening, back in my Hongō room, and heard distant *banzai* cheers for someone off to the front, I wanted desperately to go and see her. I steeled myself against it, though, because that strength of will was precisely what I aspired to. When the longing became too intense, I took the paper knife from my desk and repeatedly stabbed my palm with it. Pain alone could make me forget. But although pain may have strengthened my will, it couldn't make my heart forget.

The next morning I left the road to climb a mountain trail that offered, through the chestnut leaves, a view of Mount Asama against a clear sky. I knew well enough that this was the way to Chieko's school lodge, but I felt no special desire to go there. I was just following my footsteps wherever they might go. The trail widened where a narrow mountain path crossed it, and a little way up the slope from there I glimpsed through the trees the veranda of a two-story building. I casually made my way into the courtyard. All at once shrill laughter rang out from the veranda. Three girls, each with a sketchbook, were looking down from it. Flustered, I froze. The girls were still giggling.

"Excuse me," I said, "but may I ask, er, whether Miss Fujiki is here?"

"Miss Fujiki?" a bright voice on the veranda repeated, echoed by others—Miss Fujiki? Miss Fujiki?—inside the house. At last the answer came.

"She hasn't come yet."

I bowed quickly, did a right about-face, and started walking. Peals of merry laughter followed me. I returned to the trail and climbed to a spot that afforded a broad view. There I smoked a cigarette and gazed at the sunlit peaks of the Yatsugatake range.

Late that afternoon I was lying sprawled on the tatami when a maid from the inn slid my door open to announce a visitor. Chieko's voice, calling my name as I jumped to my feet, dispelled every shred of gloom.

"Chieko!" I answered in a voice charged with emotion.

She smiled somewhat shyly and hastily let me know that she had a friend with her. "I hope you don't mind," she added.

"Of course I don't mind. Who is it?"

"Miss Suga."

Chieko entered the room in the company of a tall, bashful girl, dressed like her in a white blouse and navy-blue skirt. I politely invited them to sit down.

"This is Suga Toshiko," Chieko announced. "She's a good friend of mine."

"Pleased to meet you," Miss Suga said.

"I've heard a lot about you," I said, smiling.

"Really? How?" She glanced at Chieko. "You've been telling tales about me, haven't you!" she said with a grin. To me she went on, "And I, Mr. Shiomi, I've heard your name almost more often than I'd care to."

"Don't, Toshiko!" Blushing, Chieko quickly sought to silence her friend. "I don't need any more of this, after the awful teasing I got today."

"Teasing? Why?" I asked.

She glowered at me.

"But, Shiomi-san," she said, "didn't you come looking for me at the lodge this morning?"

"Yes, I did. I was out for a stroll, and I just stopped by. How did you know it was me, though?"

"Oh, that was easy. They all started teasing me about it the moment I arrived."

"Look, Chieko," her friend laughed, "you needn't get *that* worked up about it. You looked pretty happy yourself. Let's just drop it."

"Fine. But you're awful!"

Embarrassed now, I changed the subject.

"When did you get here, Chieko?"

"Just a little while ago. We took the Koume Line train from Lake Yamanaka. The scenery on the way was so pretty. Don't you think so, Toshiko?"

"Oh yes. You could see Yatsugatake perfectly. I actually wanted to get off at Nobeyama and have a look around."

The two went on to each other, as though they'd completely forgotten me, about how beautiful the highland landscape had been.

They were like children. A sort of vague happiness came over me as I watched.

"Lake Yamanaka was beautiful too," Chieko said.

"So Miss Suga was with you?"

"Yes, we were together the whole time. Toshiko is a devout Christian. I learn a lot from her. I always wish I had her single-minded faith."

"But I have a long way to go yet. You really shouldn't say things like that."

"I'm always wobbly, confused, and unhappy, though. Shiomi-san here doesn't even *try* to believe. He's a hard case. Yes, he's the rock in my path."

"I don't mean to be."

"No, but you are anyway. Faith comes for me before everything else when I'm with Reverend Sawada and Toshiko, but when I'm with you it seems perfectly normal that you can't believe. It's very painful. Maybe you could help me a little, Toshiko, and try to convince him."

"Me? Why, I hardly think . . ."

"I doubt that faith is something you can give *anyone* by force of persuasion," I put in. "Once faith starts moving in you, then no doubt it helps to have someone there to guide you, but surely someone impervious to faith will just get his back up if you go on and on to him about God."

"But, Shiomi-san, I'm certain that you really *are* open to faith. What could be harder than purposely shutting yourself into your solitude, to suffer through it as you do, and to insist that it's your problem and no one else's? Why shouldn't someone that painfully disposed at least give faith a chance?"

"It's all I can do just to be what I am," I said.

"Apparently you can't bring your closest friend to faith," Toshiko observed. "You should be able to do better than that."

Chieko looked crestfallen. Beyond the window a cicada was singing away. Abruptly there was a rumbling roar, and the cicada stopped. The room shook.

"Let's go," said Chieko quietly. She was pale.

The two started out of the room, Chieko a step behind. Her eyes met mine. "Chieko," I said in a low voice, "would you come for a walk in the mountains tomorrow?"

"Just you and me?"

"Yes. You'd rather not?"

Alarm flickered over her face. She pursed her lips a little, frowned, and glanced at about the middle of my chest. Then she raised her eyes and silently nodded yes. I detected some sort of vague emotion that I hadn't noticed in her before.

From outside the inn you could see pure white smoke billowing from Mount Asama. The top of the soaring column mingled with the late afternoon clouds and drifted eastward like a plume of pampas grass. Chieko stared at it wide-eyed until her friend reminded her that they ought to go.

The next afternoon, Chieko and I left the hiking trail to follow a logging road through the forest.

Asama had been quaking ominously ever since the previous day. Through the trees came pheasants' eerie calls. Chieko was wearing a pale blue cardigan over her white blouse. She cringed every time the mountain rumbled. Out there in the woods, though, it was still. There was no one else around. Chestnuts in their green husks rustled high in the tall chestnut trees.

"Is it all right?" she asked, her eyes shining.

"Is what all right? Of course it is. We still haven't met a single bear."

I lit a cigarette and teased her about being a scaredy-cat. She was picking early autumn flowers and alpine plants along the roadside.

"I'm *not* a scaredy-cat," she retorted.

"A crybaby, then."

"I'm *not*!"

"But, Chieko, being scared of my joining the army is the reason you wanted to break up with me, isn't it?"

She glanced at my face and walked on with a downcast gaze. Gloom settled over me. Yesterday our reunion had seemed a happy miracle, but today the whole thing felt more like a point-less replay of the past. Two people meet, then part. They meet only to part—or was it just that my being alone had soured me into feeling this way? What would survive this brief rendezvous between Chieko and me? It would be all over once I went into the army. Soon no doubt I'd die miserably on a battlefield some-where while Chieko lived on, suffered, laughed, and loved some-one else. Being alive means living for yourself. It means listening to the music of Chopin, believing in God, taking the train back and forth on the Koume Line. Her being alive had nothing to do with me.

"I've thought a lot about what you said," I whispered as though to myself. "I just can't fathom why we should have to break up.

Once I'm drafted there's no knowing whether we'll ever meet again, so no wonder I want to keep seeing you at least until then! How can you be cruel enough to say we shouldn't see each other anymore?"

"But we'll only be unhappy if we go on this way," she answered very quietly.

"*I'm* happy, though. I'm deeply happy whenever I'm with you, but you . . ."

"Me, too. Even so . . ."

"Meaning that I've never been more to you than a friend who's nice to have around. When all's said and done, I've just been a stand-in for your brother, a nice sort of private tutor, useful till you grow up yourself. You've never loved me."

"Shiomi-san!" It was almost a guttural cry. "How can you say such awful things? It's just because I *do* love you that I'm suffering, too! Don't you see?"

There were tears in her voice by now. She stopped and turned her head away. The way her slender shoulders drooped made her back look terribly sad.

"It's like a knife going through me, every time you talk about how utterly alone you are, and there's absolutely nothing I can do for you."

"All I ask is that you love me."

"Love you . . . But true love comes only through love of God."

"Not as *I* see it. It's the most human of all emotions. You don't have to know God to love."

"Love is even more joyous and beautiful, though, if you *do* know God."

"All right, then by all means fall in love with a good Christian. You have no business loving a miserable character like me."

I spat out this venom in surge of anger. Chieko's back shook more.

"But I swear that no one in the world loves you as much as I do."

I took a few steps forward. Eyes still to the ground, she came up to walk beside me. In one hand she still clutched a bunch of flowers.

"Yes, I'm alone," I went on, "and to me that's a miserable condition to be in. A man alone who hates this war can still do nothing whatsoever about it. He can only cross his arms and wait to be drafted. After that he just waits to be massacred. If only there was some sort of organization around, a group of people sufficiently united in opposition to the war to be able to stop it, I'd gladly join. Then, yes, I'd give up my pitiful little solitude to fight for the common good. But where would I find an outfit like that? I know of none. They've already got all the Communists. This all-powerful police state of ours instantly stamps out the least little germ of freedom. I'm so isolated, you're really and truly the only person I can talk to about what I think. That's why this miserable little solitude of mine is so precious to me."

We climbed a gentle slope to the top of a small hill with a view of the village below and sat there side by side on the grass. A goat was bleating in a field nearby, ruts scarred the dry surface of the road, and the distant forest shone green in the sun. Fresh smoke billowed continually from the summit of Mount Asama into an infinitely high summer sky. Chieko took off her cardigan.

"Even those who believe in God," I said, "even those who feel duty-bound to love their neighbor, *they* do nothing to oppose the war, so how is anyone else supposed to? If the Christians had come right out against it, that might have done to get an opposition movement going. The Roman persecution of the early Christians, the history of Christianity in Japan—I'd say the Christians managed to put up that kind of resistance because they were *organized*. That's part of their history. But now, what with unconditional acquiescence in the war and everyone praying for the Greater Japanese Empire, the opposition of isolated individuals can make no difference at all. I don't and can't really do a thing, for all my talk. I'm a coward, as far as I'm concerned. Even *I* would gladly join this Reverend Sawada of yours, if only he'd stand up against the war. Uchimura Kanzō was put on trial for *lèse-majesté*, wasn't he, for having refused to show due respect to the emperor's portrait? Is there no one left with that kind of backbone? The Non-Church movement is just as powerless as the Church itself, really. So believing in God is no different from lying in the sun. I'd just as soon *not* believe in that kind of God. Alone like this, I'm helpless, too, but at least it seems to me I'm a hundred times more honest, more genuinely human, than those who think God is on our side. With God I might get by without suffering, but it's precisely not having him around that allows me to suffer like a man. For me, neither love nor suffering has anything to do with God."

My mouth was dry by now, and I lapsed into exhausted silence. Chieko, her folded cardigan on her lap, was gazing at the bunch of flowers in her hand. I had nothing further to say. All was quiet. The only sound was the faint, mournful bleating of the goat.

"I shouldn't have said all that," I murmured.

Chieko looked my way. Her pale, earnest gaze bored into me.

"You just won't believe in God, will you?" she said.

"No."

"So what *do* you believe in?"

"Nothing."

"You believe in nothing? You don't believe in me, either?"

"In you? Yes, I believe in you. Just you."

"But, but, the human heart is so fickle! God's love never changes, but human love comes to an end."

"Perhaps so. I've chosen you, though. That's why this heart of mine, this heart that loves you, prefers to believe in you. You're the one I've chosen."

"I see." She spoke very low, nodding.

I put my head in my hands and felt a surge of inexpressible regret. No exchange of words, however sharp, can impose one person's will on another. Chieko wasn't about to give up her faith in God, and I wasn't about to believe in God and become a Christian. And love—yes, love was presumably just an image we elaborate in our hearts to adorn our own loneliness: a capricious, self-serving dream. Back then, Fujiki Shinobu had utterly failed to understand my love, regardless of how I went about explaining it to him. Now, to his sister my burning feelings were probably no more than a profane delusion. With my dream of heavenly, eternal love I was perhaps in her eyes no more than a sinner without faith in God.

"I see," Chieko said. She handed me her cardigan and stood up. Bouquet in hand, she took a deep breath and looked straight at me. "Let's not talk about this any more," she said gently.

"I'll go and pick some more flowers," she murmured, almost to herself. She left the path and went off into the forest.

I put the pale blue cardigan on my lap, sank my fingers into its wooly warmth, and decided to stop thinking about these awful things. Beyond the forest rose, like a wall, the mottled green and brown flanks of the volcano. Cicadas sang on and off among the trees. What really matters now, I told myself, is not to dwell on future misery, but rather to merge with all this nature, all this peace. War, death, God, and so on can have nothing to do with Chieko and me as long as she picks her flowers and I watch the mountain. We're living now just as we are now. What other life could there be, beyond this now?

"Chieko!" I called.

No answer. Holding her cardigan I stood up and started after her into the forest.

It was quiet there, and I suddenly felt the chilly dampness of the leaves. Creepers threatened to trip me, and low-hanging chestnut branches barred my way. I walked on for a while but still saw no sign of Chieko. Twice I shouted her name and listened hard for a response.

A thick growth of beech, oak, chestnut oak, and pines rose high in majestic silence, with here and there among them the smooth trunk of a silver birch. Through the branches overhead poured the curiously dappled rays of the afternoon sun. I walked on a little further. The ground sloped up gently, and my feet began to feel cold.

"Chieko!" I called again.

Abruptly there was laughter nearby. I froze in astonishment while Chieko, who had been crouching behind a curtain of vines, jumped up and ran off. "Wait for me!" I shouted, racing after her. She laughed shrilly. The vine-tangled tree trunks ran, the thorny thickets ran, the whole forest tilted back and forth, left and right. Only Chieko's white blouse sped further off or came closer.

All at once she cried out and stopped. Panting, I caught up with her at last. I put my arms around her, to hold her close. In one hand she still held the flowers she'd picked, and tremulously she stretched the other toward a branch of a nearby chestnut oak.

"Look!"

A tiny animal was staring quizzically down at us from the branch.

"It's a squirrel!" I exclaimed and burst into laughter.

"I was so surprised! It jumped up right in front of me!"

The squirrel flipped its fluffy, chestnut-colored tail and gazed at us wide-eyed, as though to say, "The surprise is mine!" Then in a flash it turned and darted off along the branch. I laughed again.

"You *are* a scaredy-cat, Chieko. I was right, wasn't I!"

I still had my arms around her from the back, just as when I'd first caught up with her. My hands, resting on her breasts, could just feel their gentle, rounded warmth. Chieko wriggled and placed her free hand over mine. She gave me a shy, sidelong look.

"I've never seen a squirrel, except in a zoo!"

Loose strands of her hair brushed my cheeks. Her breasts swelled more warmly under my hands. I bent her backwards and searched for her lips.

"My flowers!" she cried. "Don't squash my flowers!"

The next moment, though, the two of us collapsed on the ground, locked in embrace. The smell of damp grass and the fresh scent of a young girl's skin filled an awareness further sparked by the touch of her warm lips. I felt for her hair, pressed it to my face. Disheveled as it was, it half hid hers. She panted hard whenever I relaxed my kiss.

So there we lay, our bodies entangled. I tried to keep her hair off the grass with one hand and placed the other over her breasts. They heaved with each breath.

"See how small they are," she said shyly.

She buried her face against me as though acutely embarrassed. Her small, warm breasts—an aspect of life I'd never known—were more than enough to inflame my passion. Desperately, I sought her lips. Our surroundings died away, leaving only us alive. Lips to lips, chest to chest, belly to belly, legs to legs, we were fused together as one. Anything felt possible then. My arms were the arms, my body the body of the possible. Unresisting she lay in my embrace, her eyes closed.

The mountain rumbled loudly. Leaves pattered down from the trees. Chieko flinched and clung to me, shaking and warmly damp with sweat. I could hardly tell whether I touched her skin directly or through her underwear. Perspiring with shame, she trembled and struggled as though her clothes were her body itself. That moment crystallized the flaming mass of my desire. Chieko was Chieko no more, but the girl in my novel: a character with a fate wholly at my disposal. And if willful desire passed to final act, then my destiny—as a living person, not as a fictional character—would be decided forever.

But something deterred me—I have no idea what. I can't remember what I was thinking. Various reasons, proximate and distant, probably lurked in the conscious and unconscious recesses of my mind, but I doubt that analysis could shed much light on them. I only know that at the last moment I faltered. And there it was: in the primeval forest of that high plateau, I couldn't become an animal. I felt no happy transport of love but, rather, a deep fear, a sort of vague flight from the thought of spiritual death. The Chieko in my arms was now a total stranger, a hallucinated invader of my inner being.

Lying there with her in my arms I found myself sequestered, alone, beyond the flow of time. This was the familiar solitude, but more intense and wretched than ever before. No blaze of passion could warm the source of the rational gaze I turned on myself. Love had not swept me off to deathlike oblivion, not even with the mountain rumbling and leaves dropping onto us from the trees. Time might have stopped forever if I'd taken that last step, but what joy would that annihilation have brought me? So I reflected. Caught between burning ardor and the void, I couldn't abolish my solitude as long as this living girl's body called me to a kind of death. Like God for Chieko, this futile solitude constituted the whole of my tiny existence. Futile, yes, it was. But it was pure.

Chieko withdrew from my embrace, turned away, and hastily tidied her clothes. Then she looked down and began collecting her flowers. I sat up. Pinks, mountain violets, and gentians lay scattered about. I went for the cardigan, which lay some way off, and put it over her shoulders. Silent, still with her back to me, Chieko let me help her on with her jacket.

"Look at these silk trees!" I said.

Several small silk trees spread their drooping branches right beside where we'd been lying. The flowers were gone, but the slender, slightly trembling branches, with their feathery leaves, cast a peaceful spell over their surroundings. If only we'd been able to love each other, to understand each other, and, beneath these trees, to start a new life together without thought or care! If only we could love each other naturally, openly, without all this agony! Nightfall would bring the silk tree leaves untroubled sleep. Seeing those little trees filled me with despair.

I remained abstracted while Chieko set off quickly through the woods, in the direction we'd come from. I started after her, but she was almost running. Obscure regrets weighed on my heart, where they multiplied in twilight profusion like the trees of an endless, primeval forest.

I didn't catch up with her till we reached the logging road. We walked on together, side by side. Behind us, the slopes of Mount Asama had turned orange in the light of the late afternoon sun. Smoke still billowed in an unbroken column from the summit. When I paused to watch it, Chieko continued on in silence. She didn't even look back. The flowers, still in her hand, were beginning to wilt.

On the road the next day I ran into Miss Suga and heard that Chieko had taken the morning train back to Tokyo.

The day after that I, too, put the Nagano highlands behind me. So ended my brief summer vacation.

A week after my return I had a short letter from Chieko. Sure enough, she said she felt we shouldn't see each other any more. I didn't answer it.

My draft notice came late that December.

I thought I'd steeled myself against this moment, in my fashion, but the red envelope pitched me into the depths of hell when the landlady handed it to me. I rushed back to my room and examined myself in the mirror: pale face, sharp features. I stared at the mirror, clouded by my cold breath, as though it threw back a stranger's face.

My first thought was of Chieko. We hadn't seen each other since that summer day. I was trying to forget her. The solitude of the hero—so I called a solitude proof against every temptation, every attack: the one toward which I continued to goad my spirit. Far be it from me to weep helplessly over the past. If Chieko had every reason to leave me, then no last-ditch effort would do anything to change her mind. Her life was hers to live, and mine was mine. The memory of our youthful love was all I wanted. With the tie between us broken, that memory, too, would no doubt slowly fade.

This had been my resolve when I returned from Oiwake to Tokyo. One evening late that autumn I ran into Suga Toshiko at Ochanomizu Station. I asked her how Chieko was getting on. With obvious embarrassment she told me that Chieko was engaged. The news felt like a slap in the face, but I quickly collected myself. I tried to maintain an air of indifference, but I'm sure my disconcerted look gave me away.

"To Yashiro?" I asked.

"No, to Mr. Ishii. Apparently Reverend Sawada is being very helpful to them."

I left her immediately, and once alone again I reflected that it was probably all for the best. I whistled as I walked. I didn't even notice that I was whistling the theme of the Chopin piano concerto.

It was Chieko I'd most wanted to see when my draft notice came—less out of love than out of friendship for a girl I'd known so long, less from desire than from nostalgia. I knew everything about her, and there was nothing she didn't know about me. That's the kind of friends we were. Now that I'd soon be off to the front, it seemed quite unnatural to go without seeing her again. Never mind who she might be engaged to—she was my closest friend, wasn't she? Besides, I wanted to see her mother, too.

I rejected these thoughts straight away, however. I'd sworn myself to a solitary life. This idea of seeing Chieko again probably came down to no more than a sentimental bid for sympathy. It merely revealed my own weakness. What good would it do me on the battlefield to have met Chieko again, seen her cheery smile, heard her somewhat high-pitched voice, and graven her image afresh on my memory? My only support was independence, imposing on myself rational conduct and a rational death. That stern principle was all I had. Yes, the problem was mine alone, and I doubt that I had any room left in me for involvement with her.

I reconsidered, though. My youth was too barren. Like my unfinished novel (it had gone nowhere since autumn, and the manuscript pages lay heaped on my desk, covered with dust), it was merely a succession of vain hopes and unrealized plans. If it was to end here and now, at my country's bidding, couldn't I at least give some brilliance to its final page? Couldn't I achieve at least that?

I meant to remain in Tokyo until the last minute and then take the night train for my hometown, where I was to report. In the newspaper I saw an ad for a piano recital to be held in Hibiya Hall on the evening of my last day. I ordered two tickets and sent one to Chieko by express post, with a short note. This was the page I had in mind to close my youth. If Chieko came, then I'd listen to Chopin with her (the program was devoted entirely to her favorite composer) and board my train. If she didn't, I'd be none the worse for it. The plan did strike me as a bit theatrical, but if it's the artist's business to compose his work beautifully, then surely it's up to him to compose reality the same way. Especially for a failed writer like me, it should be at least some comfort to write his last page if not in his novel, then at least in his life.

On the morning of my last day I went into the garden of my lodging house and burned the manuscript of my unfinished novel, together with my diary and all my notes. There on the black, frosty soil, small flames rose from the dry, crackling paper. Now and again I stirred the heap with a bamboo pole and held my numb hands to the fire. You could hear the faint drone of an airplane, high in the winter sky.

The concert was about to begin, but the seat next to mine was still empty.

Silence reigned. The lights had dimmed, and a mood of eager anticipation filled the hall. The only light was directed at the stage, where a small man in tails, seated before a blackly gleaming grand piano, began somewhat affectedly to move his hands. Chopin, too, must have been a rather affected youth. He, too, no doubt looked as though his audience meant nothing to him and kept his eyes closed, engrossed in the melodies that sprang from his hands. Waves of music, like glittering calls to life, swirled through the hall. To life? Or perhaps to death. I felt only a craving for oblivion—a fierce desire to forget the foul reality confronting me and to enclose myself entirely in the intoxication of the moment. Behind this wish for no future lay a constant anxiety.

The intermission came, but still no Chieko. A woman was taking tickets by the reception desk in the lobby, I went out to stand near her. Chieko was not among those who came rushing up to her.

Only the seat next to mine remained vacant. The empty space felt very bleak. The concert resumed. Two or three seats in front of me a young man, presumably a student, was leafing through the score. The mere rustle of the paper conveyed a hopeless sense of loss. Chieko wouldn't be coming. I pitied the childish theatricality of sending her the ticket. I should just have gone straight to her house, if I wanted to see her. Then I'd have been able to say goodbye to her mother, too. It was too late now. I could imagine various reasons why she hadn't come. In the end, though, only one of them persisted: she'd never loved me.

At the next intermission I lit a cigarette and was on my way to the reception desk when a young woman greeted me. "It's been a long time!" she said.

I remembered that smiling, girlish face. It was Suga Toshiko. Without thinking I replied, "Are you alone?"

"Yes, I am. And you?"

I nodded. The two of us started for the balcony outside. I kept wondering whether Chieko had told her the whole story. Perhaps, I thought, this Toshiko is here with a message from her.

"Chopin's music is so sweet, isn't it?" she remarked, smiling as ever.

We leaned against the railing and gazed out into the black, starless night. The trees around the square stood rigid with cold in the dim light of the streetlamps.

"Do you go to a lot of concerts?" I asked.

"Yes, I love music. You, too, Mr. Shiomi?"

"No, not that many."

"Oh, but I know you do. Chieko always says so. Actually, I believe I've run into you here before."

I'd been staring vacantly at a light blinking in the distance, but at this I suddenly realized that that smile on Toshiko's face, when she'd greeted me a few minutes ago, had had a particular meaning.

"Oh, was that *you*," I exclaimed, "that music-lover friend of Chieko's who described Chopin as sweet?"

"Yes, it was."

We both laughed. Her smile put dimples in her cheeks. It occurred to me that I hadn't laughed out loud for a very long time.

"I gather you had some hard words for me then," she said. "Chieko told me all about it."

I felt my smile turn wry.

"We ran into each other that time at Ochanomizu Station, didn't we?" I said. "Is she really engaged to Yashiro?"

"No, no, to Ishii. Did I tell you Yashiro?"

"Ah, I see. I had it wrong. So it's Ishii? I can't help it, it feels so strange that she's marrying him."

"It certainly does." Toshiko nodded, gazing out into the night. "I'd always assumed she'd marry *you*."

"That's not what I meant," I said bitterly. "I'm no good. I don't believe in God, you see."

"What? What does *that* have to do with it?" Toshiko turned to me and looked into my eyes. "If only you love somebody, surely it doesn't matter whether the person believes in God or not! Sorry, I'm talking out of turn."

The bell rang to call the audience back to their seats. The crowd around us began to stir.

"If you love somebody, yes," I repeated mockingly. "But she doesn't love me."

"That's not true!" Toshiko spoke loudly enough to turn heads.

"Then why is she marrying Ishii?"

"I don't know, but there's no doubt whatever that Chieko loves you. That was always my feeling."

I started walking. Only the lights glittered now in the all but empty lobby.

"I'm no good," I said again, looking straight ahead as we walked on, side by side. "Besides, I've received my draft notice. I'm just about to go."

"You are? Really? When?" She put her hand on my arm.

"Tonight. I'm taking the night train. So I'll say good-bye."

Without looking back I pushed open the door and entered the concert hall. It was already in semidarkness. The piano's clear notes began floating down from the stage just as I reached my seat. The seat next to me was still empty.

I had no thoughts. I didn't even wonder what it would have been like if Chieko, rather than Toshiko, had come. I was sorry not to have seen her, but I fully intended now to forget about that, too. I did my best to look as happy as everyone else in the audience as they watched the pianist and immersed themselves in that sweet, sweet music. Among these people, I said to myself, there must also be pairs of lovers; there must also be breasts atremble with thoughts of love even sweeter than Chopin's melodies. Well, let them be happy, then. By all means, let as many people as possible be untroubled and happy in love. One day the war will be over and peace will return. Till then, only let the serious eyes of youths entranced by music, and the warm smiles of girls whose every breath is love, not be lost from the earth. I just wish you all happiness . . .

The concert program ended, then the encores. The departing crowd swept me out of the hall and out into the brightly lit corridor where a pale Suga Toshiko was waiting.

"You didn't have to wait for me, Miss Suga!" I said.
Toshiko walked with me toward the exit. "Are you really leaving tonight?" she asked.

"Yes. I'm off right now to Tokyo Station."

"But what about Chieko? Will she be waiting for you at the station?"

"I hardly think so. She doesn't even know what time the train leaves."

We descended the steps and came out onto the dim square. The air was cold and dry. I'd been with Chieko the last time I'd heard Chopin. It had been late spring. I thought back to that time.

"Have you seen her at all?" Toshiko inquired.

"No, not for a long time. How has she been?"

"Why didn't you go to say good-bye to her?" Toshiko's tone was puzzled and accusing. "I just don't understand."

I said nothing. We walked on toward Yūrakuchō Station.

"She's lost weight recently," she said in a low voice. "The last two or three days she's stayed home from school. She says it's a cold or something."

"Really? A cold?" I answered with a little more life in my voice. She couldn't come this evening, I told myself, because she's ill. The thought made me feel better.

At Yūrakuchō Toshiko insisted on seeing me all the way to Tokyo Station, but I said no.

"I don't want anyone to see me off," I explained, smiling. "Look at me—I spent my last evening at a concert. I'm not quite like other people."

"Are you sure? It just doesn't feel right."

"It *is* all right, though. Thank you. I feel a little better for having met you. Be well."

"Good-bye, then. Please look after yourself. I'll pray for your success in battle."

"Good-bye. Say hello to Chieko for me. Tell her to get over her cold soon."

Toshiko, moist-eyed, managed to give me a smile and headed for the ticket gate. I watched her go and then strolled off alone along the Ginza. It was still a little early for the train. Hands thrust deep in my overcoat pockets, I peered into the display windows as though I hadn't a care in the world. Christmas was coming, but the Ginza felt nowhere near as lively as it had been in my student days. Among the pedestrians there were many soldiers. They'd suddenly straighten up and salute whenever they met an officer. In their clumsy manner I saw my own future. Loudspeakers on the storefronts blared martial songs out into the street.

I went back to Yūrakuchō Station, picked up the suitcase I'd left at the checkroom, and headed for Tokyo Station.

The brightly lit platform was crowded with people seeing passengers off. Almost all were bidding farewell to young army draftees. They stood in circles, each clutching a little Japanese flag, singing army songs. At rigid attention in the middle of each circle, with an indescribable look on his face, stood a man wearing a red shoulder-to-waist sash across his chest. It was a great relief to have refused any such ceremony. It would have been quite unbearable.

To my confusion and embarrassment a young officer with a saber at his side came up to me. It was Tachibana, my friend from the science course in high school. Some of those I'd been with at the archery camp were now employed in the provinces, and some had joined the army. Only Tachibana had stayed on in Tokyo, where he was now assigned to Air Force Headquarters. I'd called him to say good-bye. It had never occurred to me that he might want to see me off.

"Why are you here?" I asked. "Aren't you too busy?"

"Why? What a question! Don't be silly! Of course I'm here!"

"But I don't like all this hoopla."

"Don't worry. I won't start singing any songs."

We talked next to a pillar. When the train pulled into the station, he took my suitcase in to find me a seat.

"Just make sure you don't die," he said. "Dying is the stupidest thing you can do. Look after Number One. And any little glitch that comes your way, take advantage of it. And keep your eyes open."

"Thanks," I said.

He told me a few stories to illustrate what he meant by looking after Number One. Tachibana hadn't changed a bit since high school. He looked pretty funny with a solemn military cap on his head instead of the white-banded one he'd worn back then. In those days, too, he'd always looked out for me and very discreetly offered me real friendship.

The bell rang to announce the train's imminent departure. He left the carriage and watched me through the window, grinning. I opened the window and grasped his hand.

"I'll see you," he said. "Keep well."

"Right, you too."

"*Banzai!*" shouts arose from here and there on the platform. Tachibana saluted when the train began to move. I waved back for a while and then closed the window. It was hot and steamy in the carriage, but I put my overcoat collar up.

In no time the train reached Shinagawa. When it pulled out again I wiped the steamed-up window with my handkerchief, pressed my face to the glass, and intently watched the lights glide past in the dark. The tip of my nose against the glass was so cold it hurt.

It was night, and I couldn't tell exactly where we were. Trying to pick out the light of a single small apartment wasn't easy. In fact, it was all but impossible. I held my breath. I did spot it, though. I thought I did. The tiny glow of Chieko's window burned itself for a moment into my retina and then, like a shooting star, was gone. The lights out there kept gliding by.

I recalled the phosphorescent creatures I'd seen in the sea at Heda, glittering in the thrust and retreat of the waves. And I remembered Fujiki Shinobu whispering faintly, "It'd be so miserable to die alone."

Fujiki! I called silently. Fujiki, you never loved me, and your sister didn't, either. And now I'm probably going to die alone . . .

I stayed on and on at the window, my face pressed to the cold glass, while the train picked up speed.

Spring

The long winter passed, and spring came.

Winter *was* long that year. Spring could have arrived at any moment, but even in March the temperature remained below freezing for days in a row, and every morning the water in our sputum cups was frozen. During the day, the frost melting on the paths turned them to mud. When at last the winds announcing the new season shook the trees, the sky filled with yellow dust that covered even our beds with grit. The patients lay there with the potted hothouse plants and whatnot on their bedside tables, the covers pulled all the way up to their heads. The winter, when there was nothing to do but stay in bed, was far better for a convalescent's health. For most of us, though, only warm sunshine helped, and we longed to be out in the sun. A glimmer of hope lit up the eyes of even the worst of the patients when the plum grove flowered, new grass sprang up, and barley stretched visibly skyward. That's how eagerly we looked forward to spring.

On fine days I made my way through the cluster of fresh-air pavilions and took the path around the back of the sanatorium. The growing barley was a vigorous green, the earth was black, and the trees in the wood were bursting into new leaf. I walked straight on to where the path crossed a channel of water to control grass fires. Six feet or so wide, it had been dug as an irrigation canal in the early nineteenth century, and it still ran lazily through the fields as a reminder of what the Musashi Plain had looked like long ago. Mount Sankaku rose beside it—just a little hill, really, but for the likes of us it was a breathless climb to the top. From there you could look through the trees to the nearby barley fields, the woods around them, and, in those woods, the roof of the sanatorium.

Sometimes I crossed the precarious stone bridge over the canal and went on a little further. Then I'd sit down on the grass and contemplate, below the gently descending slope, the farmhouses among their windbreak trees, the rivulets, and the little temple, sleeping in the sunshine. All this made a refreshing, touchingly peaceful scene.

My walk often took me that far. Sometimes I went by myself, or Kaku came with me. Mostly I was alone, though. I'd gaze at the canal's brimming flow, and now and again I'd bend down to dip my hand into it. The water was now gradually warming up. I'd make a bamboo-leaf boat and launch it from the end of the bridge, just as I'd done when I was a child. Around and around it would spin, now glancing off the bank, now catching on the waterweeds, until it disappeared downstream. At times like these my heart seemed to swell with the joy of living. All sorts of feelings ran through me.

Shiomi Shigeshi's death especially, and the reason for it, lurked somehow menacingly deep within me.

One day while the snow was melting I'd gone to the mortuary and read those two notebooks filled with his small, closely packed handwriting. I couldn't make up my mind, though, whether his death was a kind of premeditated suicide or simply a case of failed surgery. Certainly it was possible to guess at his reason for writing, but I still had no idea what had been on his mind before he died, or why he had given them to me. I allowed myself to imagine that on the battlefield he'd been unable to preserve the integrity of his solitude and so had taken a strong dislike to himself. But what was to be gained from such speculation? Of his own free will he'd chosen either death or an operation that put his life at risk. He'd had no regrets. He'd kept that independence of his intact, and none of us could have anything further to say about it.

Shiomi spoke to me a few days before the operation. "Once I was afraid of death," he said. "There was so much that I didn't want to lose. Love, happiness, youth, ambition—things like that, you know. Now I have only myself to lose, and this self of mine is what I dislike most."

In hindsight, he'd definitely decided by then to die; but he seemed so utterly untroubled that I never guessed. I immediately forgot those words of his, among many others. While I roamed beside the canal, however, Shiomi's casual, half-forgotten remark came to me through the murmuring of the water.

His ashes returned to his home, in his brother's care. The two notebooks stayed behind with me. I borrowed the membership list of his high school alumni association, looked up the names of his friends, and notified them of his death. Thanks to this correspondence I learned sometime later the address of Ishii Chieko.

I couldn't decide whether to let her read what he'd written. In all likelihood she was happily married somewhere in the country. No doubt her relationship with Shiomi now belonged to the distant past. I had no wish to disturb the peace of someone else's life. Still, conjecture about what he'd had in mind made it seem likely that, for him, the reader best able to understand what he'd written was the only woman he'd ever loved.

After long hesitation, I wrote at last to Chieko. I explained my connection with Shiomi Shigeshi and told her how he'd died. I also gave her a detailed account of the notebooks he'd left, adding that I'd send them immediately if she had any wish to read them. After I mailed the letter, I sometimes felt I should never have done it.

No answer came. Spring was already well along when at last it arrived. The heavy envelope bore many stamps. There was something moving about her fine writing, done with a pen.

I read Chieko's long letter on the grass beyond the canal. It had been winter when I read Shiomi's notebooks, and now the air was warm. Grass was growing, and everywhere dandelions were out. Up in the sky, larks were singing madly while scattered white clouds floated gently by. This is what she had written.

> Thank you for your letter. It was a very sad one.
>
> I have not forgotten Mr. Shiomi. I did try to, though. It is just that in the end I had to give up. When your letter came, and I saw that it was from someone unknown to me, I wondered what could possibly be in it. Then I unfolded the paper, and when I saw the name Shiomi

Shigeshi my hand began trembling so much that I had to put it down. You may laugh, but it was not fear. It is more that I had heard next to nothing about him after he was drafted. When I graduated from my women's college I married Mr. Ishii, and we soon had a child. In the year the war ended my husband found a position in a high school, and ever since then I have been cooped up here in the countryside. I assumed all the time that Mr. Shiomi had been safely discharged and was alive and well somewhere. He had always wanted to write, and I looked forward to reading something good by him. I got into the habit of going into every bookstore I passed, to check the contents of the literary magazines. I so wanted him to do well, you see. It never for a moment occurred to me that he was ill and under care in a sanatorium, so how could I have ever imagined him dying a lonely death? The shock of reading your letter stopped my breath and set my hands shaking. Shiomi was dead: the impact of the news made it all too clear how much he meant to me. If only I had known, before, that he was ill! I felt such intense regret that I simply did not know what to do with myself. However, I have a husband and a daughter, and in the end I doubt that I could have done much for him. I owe you my heartfelt thanks. The past is the past. Shiomi was always so solitary. Your friendship must have been a great comfort to him during his illness. He was not a happy man.

Perhaps you imagine me living a happy life. I used to believe that he and I would be happy if we just each followed our own path, but that was long ago. I cannot imagine him ever being happy later on. And I, a housewife with a child, I have had my troubles, too. Still, my life certainly looks peaceful and happy enough. Now and again, though, when I listen to Setsuko playing with her dolls, or when I put the clothes my husband has left lying about back on their hangers, I suddenly find myself wondering whether my life now hasn't been a terrible mistake, and my heart feels unbearably empty. We are lucky to enjoy here the mild climate of the Tōkai region. The trees in the garden are covered in new leaves, and the wisteria and azaleas are in full bloom, but I still go out sometimes into a neglected corner of the garden to stand there, for how long I hardly know, sick at heart with an inexpressible anguish. I have known sorrow, and I have seen and heard how cruel the world can be. I suspect that as we age we retain only our trials and tribulations, and little by little forget everything happy or beautiful from our past. But I should not run on like this. None of it need concern you.

You ask why I broke with Mr. Shiomi. I have no wish to defend myself. If happiness really was impossible for him, then the fault was mine. However, I simply could not understand his artistic temperament, and I always believed that his being with an ordinary woman like me would only lead to unhappiness for us both. It is easy to talk about happiness or unhappiness, but I doubt that either really means much in relation to a burning passion. I had not grasped that, then. Besides, I wanted to be loved as the flesh and blood person I really am. It was extremely painful to realize that what he saw in me was an ideal. I am entirely ordinary. In my ordinariness, however, he saw something extraordinary. He was bound to wake up from his fantasy sooner or later. I used to feel a chill go through me at the thought that one day he would become disenchanted with me. He was a dreamer, and reality is all I know.

I was a devout Christian when I suggested to him that we should part. My two loves were on different levels, but I believed that my love of God and my love for Shiomi could coexist in me. However, God is a hard master, and I became increasingly certain that I would have to choose between them. Shiomi did not believe in God. It seemed to me that co-existence would be possible if loving me could bring him even a tiny bit closer to faith. However, he was too stubborn. He always kept to himself. And I, on my side, did not want to lose my faith.

I was reading Luther then. I realized that the essence of sin is to seek God for the sake of one's own happiness. I took "one's own happiness" in my case to mean my love for Shiomi. The greater the purity of that love, the more acutely I felt my own impurity, and the more earnestly I felt compelled to seek God. Luther says over and over again that the essence of repentance is not loving another for oneself, but giving that other pure love for the other's sake. That was my dilemma. When I felt strong, it seemed to me that if I really loved him, then for his own sake I should remove myself from him; and when I felt weak, the only way to live seemed to be to make myself strong by clinging to God. Either way, the more I loved him, the more true love meant leaving him. It was very painful. No letter came from him all summer, and I prayed every day to overcome my loneliness. That August I attended Reverend Sawada's Bible study gathering at Lake Yamanaka, where the very blue of the lake and sky made it impossible for me to stop thinking of him. I tried to convince myself that this weakness of mine was due to the inadequacy of my prayers. However, you cannot deceive your own heart. I yearned far less for the invisible God than I did for the all too visible Shiomi. It pained me extremely that this yearning had to do with my happiness only, not his. By the time my friend Suga Toshiko and I reached the Oiwake lodge in late August, I was halfway toward regretting my former resolve.

And there I met him, half by chance, but also half as I had expected. We again took up our old, interminable discussions, and I saw clearly how much he loved me. I forgot all about God. I was quite content to give up the peace of my own poor little soul if I really could make him happy. He called me an egoist. I am sure that he was right. At the time I would have abandoned my God without regret if only Shiomi had wanted me to. You will probably think that shallow of me. The way Mount Asama was erupting frightened me, and, beyond that, I feared the unknown. However, it is not that my egoism recoiled from the unknown. The two of us could have burned in hell, for all I cared.

I am sure he looked down on me for feeling that way. Late that afternoon we came down from the mountain without having done anything irrevocable. The setting sun bathed the mountains in a red glow. I felt then that our hearts were too far apart. At the same time, I hastened to prostrate myself before God and confess my all-too-susceptible weakness. Now that Shiomi had refrained from choosing me, it seemed to me that God had chosen me instead. No doubt this was purely self-serving egoism on my part. Perhaps it would also not be entirely untrue, though, to say that I had had enough anguish. After brief hesitation I accepted my husband's proposal of marriage. Fed up with my own will, I half threw myself instead on the will of God. I chose my husband freely, however, not in deference to my mother or Reverend Sawada. If I have failed to be happy since then, that, too, is something for which I alone am responsible. Neither my mother nor my husband is to blame in any way.

I never knew that Shiomi had received his draft notice. I had been out of school for a week with a cold. Only on my return did I learn from Suga Toshiko that he was now in the army. This came as a shock, and everything seemed to go dark as she spoke. I went home and told my mother in tears what had happened. Why didn't he let me know? I cried. I will never forget the look on my mother's face. She said that an express letter had come from him, but that she had opened it herself because I was unwell. Worried that my cold might get worse, she had planned to go to the concert in my place, but she dropped the idea when my fever went up that evening, and in the end she kept the whole thing to herself. I was furious, I cried, I called her names. Cold or no cold, fever or no fever, I wished I had gone to say good-bye to him. From my mother's perspective, though, I was already engaged, and I suppose she just could not bring herself to give me the letter. I still remember it. It was just a note—one very like him:

> Chieko, my draft notice has come at last. I mean to spend my last evening at a concert and then take the night train back to my hometown. I've enclosed a ticket. If you come you'll make me very happy. We're such old friends, after all.
> Please say hello to your mother for me.

I burned the letter with all the others when I got married, but the ticket, faded now, is still there, slipped into my Bible. You may smile at me for being childishly sentimental. At the time I wept, clinging to my mother's knees, with the letter and ticket from him still in my hand. That is how it happened that I never saw him again.

I have written too much already. What more could I possibly say? I suspected vaguely then, and far more clearly now, that Mr. Shiomi loved not the person I actually am but, through me, something eternal, something pure, something feminine. That eternity was, I think, the God in whom he could never believe; that purity, my brother; and that essential feminine essence an ideal not unlike Goethe's "eternal woman." It occurred to me sometimes that Shiomi looked at me with the same eyes that had looked at my brother, and that he thought of him when he saw me. I loved my brother very much. He really did have a pure, beautiful soul. Yes, he died young, but he lived on in Shiomi's heart.

I could not imagine myself ever equaling my brother in any way. My mother often said the same thing. His death was a catastrophe, but I think that it at least freed me from feeling inferior. However, Shiomi never forgot my brother, and his constant scrutiny, comparing the two of us on every point, gradually became more than I could bear. When I was in love with Shiomi, I felt the brother I had lost somehow present in his shadow, and I hated him. "Hate" is a hard word, but I have no wish to prettify my feelings. Shiomi and I both lived under the spell of my brother, who was no longer even of this world. That is probably one of the reasons that drew me away from Shiomi and moved me to accept my husband's proposal. In that sense, my husband lives completely outside my brother's influence.

At the moment I am scrimping and saving to have Set-suko learn the piano. There is a piano school not far from where we live. Sometimes, while waiting for her, I lean against the fence and listen to the practicing going on inside. Whenever I hear one of the better students play a Chopin fantasy or waltz, the sweet melody pierces my heart, and the past lives again before my eyes. I wonder how Shiomi felt when he died. No, no one knows what lies in the depths of the human heart. My own feelings are difficult enough to explain clearly. My fate is one that I chose myself, but I doubt that anyone but God knows what it means.

I have written this long, long letter just as the words came to me. Thank you very much indeed for your kindness. I pray that you recover as quickly as possible. Please keep everything that Shiomi wrote. I expect reading it would only bring back vain regrets.

I hope you can forgive me.

Translator's Afterword

Born on the southern island of Kyushu in 1918, Takehiko Fukunaga (in Japanese, Fukunaga Takehiko) attended Tokyo Imperial University, where he studied French literature. A great admirer of Western literature and classics, which he read in the original languages, he also translated several early Japanese classics into modern Japanese. He made his name above all as a novelist, but he also published poetry and literary criticism, as well as a number of detective stories.

Fukunaga's literary career began in the immediate postwar period, which Donald Keene described this way:

> Some writers lived in dire poverty and others were tormented by doubts concerning the kind of writing it behooved them to pursue, but all were sure that to be a writer was a worthy calling for men of the new Japan.

Surely no writer of the time believed more deeply than Fukunaga in the dignity and value of literature as a profession. This faith shows through clearly in *Flowers of Grass* (*Kusa no hana*, 1954), his best-known work.

Fukunaga was able to pursue his literary interests during the war because poor health excused him from military service. In July 1945 the poet Akiko Harajō (b. 1923) bore him a son, the distinguished contemporary writer Natsuki Ikezawa. In the same year he moved to Hokkaido in order to seek treatment for tuberculosis as well as to escape the air raids. In 1947 he underwent surgery and spent six years, from then to 1953, in a sanatorium at Kiyose, north of Tokyo. The opening section of *Flowers of Grass* distills personal experience.

Christianity, too, figures in *Flowers of Grass*, the title of which comes from the Bible. Fukunaga's mother was an active Christian, and he went to church regularly as a child. After drifting away from Christianity, he became a practicing Christian again two years before he died. He received baptism on his deathbed in 1979.

Fukunaga published his first story in 1946 and his first novel in 1952, but it was *Flowers of Grass,* two years later, that established his reputation. More novels and story collections followed in the late fifties and in the sixties. *The Island of Death* (*Shi no shima*, 1971), his last novel, evokes the last twenty-four hours in a man's life before the atomic bombing of Hiroshima. It won the Japan Literature Prize (*Nihon Bungaku Shō*) and has drawn high praise from some critics. However, like all Fukunaga's novels except *Flowers of Grass*, it is now out of print.

Fukunaga was released from the sanitarium in March 1953 and wrote *Flowers of Grass* between summer and Christmas of that year. He called it "a novel of lost youth" and wrote that it summed up all he had thought and felt, up to the age of about twenty. He also saw it as a sort of graduation thesis. He described it as "unusually auto-biographical," since in principle he disapproved of autobiographical novels, but he also took care to specify that all the incidents in it were pure fiction. "I don't know how to row a boat like that," he wrote, "and I can't swim." Still, he did belong to his high-school archery club, and he sought inspiration from a group photograph of its members for his characters in that part of the book.

Japan is no longer what it was in 1954, and the issues of the day have changed. *Flowers of Grass* may not be as widely read as it once was, but there are still contemporary readers who find it deeply moving. The struggle between love and irreducible human solitude goes on, after all. As one distinguished literary scholar said in Tokyo, when I mentioned that I was translating it, "Oh yes, *Flowers of Grass*! We all used to read and reread that book! It was our story."

TAKEHIKO FUKUNAGA, novelist and poet, was born in Fukuoka, Japan, in 1918. Following in the footsteps of his idols Baudelaire, Mallarmé, Rimbaud, and Lautréamont, his books are famous for their dark, often experimental edge, but Fukunaga was also known to write crime novels under a pseudonym. He died in 1979.

ROYALL TYLER, now retired, has taught Japanese language and culture at Ohio State University, the University of Wisconsin, the University of Oslo, and the Australian National University.

PETROS ABATZOGLOU, *What Does Mrs. Freeman Want?*
MICHAL AJVAZ, *The Golden Age.*
The Other City.
PIERRE ALBERT-BIROT, *Grabinoulor.*
YUZ ALESHKOVSKY, *Kangaroo.*
FELIPE ALFAU, *Chromos.*
Locos.
JOÃO ALMINO, *The Book of Emotions.*
IVAN ÂNGELO, *The Celebration.*
The Tower of Glass.
DAVID ANTIN, *Talking.*
ANTÓNIO LOBO ANTUNES, *Knowledge of Hell.*
The Splendor of Portugal.
ALAIN ARIAS-MISSON, *Theatre of Incest.*
IFTIKHAR ARIF AND WAQAS KHWAJA, EDS., *Modern Poetry of Pakistan.*
JOHN ASHBERY AND JAMES SCHUYLER, *A Nest of Ninnies.*
ROBERT ASHLEY, *Perfect Lives.*
GABRIELA AVIGUR-ROTEM, *Heatwave and Crazy Birds.*
HEIMRAD BÄCKER, *transcript.*
DJUNA BARNES, *Ladies Almanack.*
Ryder.
JOHN BARTH, *LETTERS.*
Sabbatical.
DONALD BARTHELME, *The King.*
Paradise.
SVETISLAV BASARA, *Chinese Letter.*
MIQUEL BAUÇÀ, *The Siege in the Room.*
RENÉ BELLETTO, *Dying.*
MAREK BIEŃCZYK, *Transparency.*
MARK BINELLI, *Sacco and Vanzetti Must Die!*
ANDREI BITOV, *Pushkin House.*
ANDREJ BLATNIK, *You Do Understand.*
LOUIS PAUL BOON, *Chapel Road.*
My Little War.
Summer in Termuren.
ROGER BOYLAN, *Killoyle.*
IGNÁCIO DE LOYOLA BRANDÃO, *Anonymous Celebrity.*
The Good-Bye Angel.
Teeth under the Sun.
Zero.
BONNIE BREMSER, *Troia: Mexican Memoirs.*
CHRISTINE BROOKE-ROSE, *Amalgamemnon.*
BRIGID BROPHY, *In Transit.*
MEREDITH BROSNAN, *Mr. Dynamite.*
GERALD L. BRUNS, *Modern Poetry and the Idea of Language.*
EVGENY BUNIMOVICH AND J. KATES, EDS., *Contemporary Russian Poetry: An Anthology.*
GABRIELLE BURTON, *Heartbreak Hotel.*
MICHEL BUTOR, *Degrees.*
Mobile.
Portrait of the Artist as a Young Ape.
G. CABRERA INFANTE, *Infante's Inferno.*
Three Trapped Tigers.
JULIETA CAMPOS, *The Fear of Losing Eurydice.*
ANNE CARSON, *Eros the Bittersweet.*
ORLY CASTEL-BLOOM, *Dolly City.*
CAMILO JOSÉ CELA, *Christ versus Arizona.*
The Family of Pascual Duarte.
The Hive.
LOUIS-FERDINAND CÉLINE, *Castle to Castle.*
Conversations with Professor Y.
London Bridge.

Normance.
North.
Rigadoon.
MARIE CHAIX, *The Laurels of Lake Constance.*
HUGO CHARTERIS, *The Tide Is Right.*
JEROME CHARYN, *The Tar Baby.*
ERIC CHEVILLARD, *Demolishing Nisard.*
LUIS CHITARRONI, *The No Variations.*
MARC CHOLODENKO, *Mordechai Schamz.*
JOSHUA COHEN, *Witz.*
EMILY HOLMES COLEMAN, *The Shutter of Snow.*
ROBERT COOVER, *A Night at the Movies.*
STANLEY CRAWFORD, *Log of the S.S. The Mrs Unguentine.*
Some Instructions to My Wife.
ROBERT CREELEY, *Collected Prose.*
RENÉ CREVEL, *Putting My Foot in It.*
RALPH CUSACK, *Cadenza.*
SUSAN DAITCH, *L.C.*
Storytown.
NICHOLAS DELBANCO, *The Count of Concord.*
Sherbrookes.
NIGEL DENNIS, *Cards of Identity.*
PETER DIMOCK, *A Short Rhetoric for Leaving the Family.*
ARIEL DORFMAN, *Konfidenz.*
COLEMAN DOWELL, *The Houses of Children.*
Island People.
Too Much Flesh and Jabez.
ARKADII DRAGOMOSHCHENKO, *Dust.*
RIKKI DUCORNET, *The Complete Butcher's Tales.*
The Fountains of Neptune.
The Jade Cabinet.
The One Marvelous Thing.
Phosphor in Dreamland.
The Stain.
The Word "Desire."
WILLIAM EASTLAKE, *The Bamboo Bed.*
Castle Keep.
Lyric of the Circle Heart.
JEAN ECHENOZ, *Chopin's Move.*
STANLEY ELKIN, *A Bad Man.*
Boswell: A Modern Comedy.
Criers and Kibitzers, Kibitzers and Criers.
The Dick Gibson Show.
The Franchiser.
George Mills.
The Living End.
The MacGuffin.
The Magic Kingdom.
Mrs. Ted Bliss.
The Rabbi of Lud.
Van Gogh's Room at Arles.
FRANÇOIS EMMANUEL, *Invitation to a Voyage.*
ANNIE ERNAUX, *Cleaned Out.*
SALVADOR ESPRIU, *Ariadne in the Grotesque Labyrinth.*
LAUREN FAIRBANKS, *Muzzle Thyself.*
Sister Carrie.
LESLIE A. FIEDLER, *Love and Death in the American Novel.*
JUAN FILLOY, *Faction.*
Op Oloop.
ANDY FITCH, *Pop Poetics.*
GUSTAVE FLAUBERT, *Bouvard and Pécuchet.*
KASS FLEISHER, *Talking out of School.*

FOR A FULL LIST OF PUBLICATIONS, VISIT:
www.dalkeyarchive.com

SELECTED DALKEY ARCHIVE TITLES

FORD MADOX FORD,
  The March of Literature.
JON FOSSE, *Aliss at the Fire.*
  Melancholy.
MAX FRISCH, *I'm Not Stiller.*
  Man in the Holocene.
CARLOS FUENTES, *Christopher Unborn.*
  Distant Relations.
  Terra Nostra.
  Vlad.
  Where the Air Is Clear.
TAKEHIKO FUKUNAGA, *Flowers of Grass.*
WILLIAM GADDIS, *J R.*
  The Recognitions.
JANICE GALLOWAY, *Foreign Parts.*
  The Trick Is to Keep Breathing.
WILLIAM H. GASS, *Cartesian Sonata*
  and Other Novellas.
  Finding a Form.
  A Temple of Texts.
  The Tunnel.
  Willie Masters' Lonesome Wife.
GÉRARD GAVARRY, *Hoppla! 1 2 3.*
  Making a Novel.
ETIENNE GILSON,
  The Arts of the Beautiful.
  Forms and Substances in the Arts.
C. S. GISCOMBE, *Giscome Road.*
  Here.
  Prairie Style.
DOUGLAS GLOVER, *Bad News of the Heart.*
  The Enamoured Knight.
WITOLD GOMBROWICZ,
  A Kind of Testament.
PAULO EMÍLIO SALES GOMES, *P's Three*
  Women.
KAREN ELIZABETH GORDON, *The Red Shoes.*
GEORGI GOSPODINOV, *Natural Novel.*
JUAN GOYTISOLO, *Count Julian.*
  Exiled from Almost Everywhere.
  Juan the Landless.
  Makbara.
  Marks of Identity.
PATRICK GRAINVILLE, *The Cave of Heaven.*
HENRY GREEN, *Back.*
  Blindness.
  Concluding.
  Doting.
  Nothing.
JACK GREEN, *Fire the Bastards!*
JIŘÍ GRUŠA, *The Questionnaire.*
GABRIEL GUDDING,
  Rhode Island Notebook.
MELA HARTWIG, *Am I a Redundant*
  Human Being?
JOHN HAWKES, *The Passion Artist.*
  Whistlejacket.
ELIZABETH HEIGHWAY, ED., *Best of*
  Contemporary Fiction from Georgia.
ALEKSANDAR HEMON, ED.,
  Best European Fiction.
AIDAN HIGGINS, *Balcony of Europe.*
  A Bestiary.
  Blind Man's Bluff
  Bornholm Night-Ferry.
  Darkling Plain: Texts for the Air.
  Flotsam and Jetsam.
  Langrishe, Go Down.
  Scenes from a Receding Past.
  Windy Arbours.
KEIZO HINO, *Isle of Dreams.*
KAZUSHI HOSAKA, *Plainsong.*

ALDOUS HUXLEY, *Antic Hay.*
  Crome Yellow.
  Point Counter Point.
  Those Barren Leaves.
  Time Must Have a Stop.
NAOYUKI II, *The Shadow of a Blue Cat.*
MIKHAIL IOSSEL AND JEFF PARKER, EDS.,
  Amerika: Russian Writers View the
  United States.
DRAGO JANČAR, *The Galley Slave.*
GERT JONKE, *The Distant Sound.*
  Geometric Regional Novel.
  Homage to Czerny.
  The System of Vienna.
JACQUES JOUET, *Mountain R.*
  Savage.
  Upstaged.
CHARLES JULIET, *Conversations with*
  Samuel Beckett and Bram van
  Velde.
MIEKO KANAI, *The Word Book.*
YORAM KANIUK, *Life on Sandpaper.*
HUGH KENNER, *The Counterfeiters.*
  Flaubert, Joyce and Beckett:
  The Stoic Comedians.
  Joyce's Voices.
DANILO KIŠ, *The Attic.*
  Garden, Ashes.
  The Lute and the Scars
  Psalm 44.
  A Tomb for Boris Davidovich.
ANITA KONKKA, *A Fool's Paradise.*
GEORGE KONRÁD, *The City Builder.*
TADEUSZ KONWICKI, *A Minor Apocalypse.*
  The Polish Complex.
MENIS KOUMANDAREAS, *Koula.*
ELAINE KRAF, *The Princess of 72nd Street.*
JIM KRUSOE, *Iceland.*
AYŞE KULIN, *Farewell: A Mansion in*
  Occupied Istanbul.
EWA KURYLUK, *Century 21.*
EMILIO LASCANO TEGUI, *On Elegance*
  While Sleeping.
ERIC LAURRENT, *Do Not Touch.*
HERVÉ LE TELLIER, *The Sextine Chapel.*
  A Thousand Pearls (for a Thousand
  Pennies)
VIOLETTE LEDUC, *La Bâtarde.*
EDOUARD LEVÉ, *Autoportrait.*
  Suicide.
MARIO LEVI, *Istanbul Was a Fairy Tale.*
SUZANNE JILL LEVINE, *The Subversive*
  Scribe: Translating Latin
  American Fiction.
DEBORAH LEVY, *Billy and Girl.*
  Pillow Talk in Europe and Other
  Places.
JOSÉ LEZAMA LIMA, *Paradiso.*
ROSA LIKSOM, *Dark Paradise.*
OSMAN LINS, *Avalovara.*
  The Queen of the Prisons of Greece.
ALF MAC LOCHLAINN,
  The Corpus in the Library.
  Out of Focus.
RON LOEWINSOHN, *Magnetic Field(s).*
MINA LOY, *Stories and Essays of Mina Loy.*
BRIAN LYNCH, *The Winner of Sorrow.*
D. KEITH MANO, *Take Five.*
MICHELINE AHARONIAN MARCOM,
  The Mirror in the Well.
BEN MARCUS,
  The Age of Wire and String.

WALLACE MARKFIELD,
Teitlebaum's Window.
To an Early Grave.
DAVID MARKSON, *Reader's Block.*
Springer's Progress.
Wittgenstein's Mistress.
CAROLE MASO, *AVA.*
LADISLAV MATEJKA AND KRYSTYNA
POMORSKA, EDS.,
Readings in Russian Poetics:
Formalist and Structuralist Views.
HARRY MATHEWS,
The Case of the Persevering Maltese:
Collected Essays.
Cigarettes.
The Conversions.
The Human Country: New and
Collected Stories.
The Journalist.
My Life in CIA.
Singular Pleasures.
The Sinking of the Odradek
Stadium.
Tlooth.
20 Lines a Day.
JOSEPH MCELROY,
Night Soul and Other Stories.
THOMAS MCGONIGLE,
Going to Patchogue.
ROBERT L. MCLAUGHLIN, ED., *Innovations:*
An Anthology of Modern &
Contemporary Fiction.
ABDELWAHAB MEDDEB, *Talismano.*
GERHARD MEIER, *Isle of the Dead.*
HERMAN MELVILLE, *The Confidence-Man.*
AMANDA MICHALOPOULOU, *I'd Like.*
STEVEN MILLHAUSER, *The Barnum Museum.*
In the Penny Arcade.
RALPH J. MILLS, JR., *Essays on Poetry.*
MOMUS, *The Book of Jokes.*
CHRISTINE MONTALBETTI, *The Origin of Man.*
Western.
OLIVE MOORE, *Spleen.*
NICHOLAS MOSLEY, *Accident.*
Assassins.
Catastrophe Practice.
Children of Darkness and Light.
Experience and Religion.
A Garden of Trees.
God's Hazard.
The Hesperides Tree.
Hopeful Monsters.
Imago Bird.
Impossible Object.
Inventing God.
Judith.
Look at the Dark.
Natalie Natalia.
Paradoxes of Peace.
Serpent.
Time at War.
The Uses of Slime Mould:
Essays of Four Decades.
WARREN MOTTE,
Fables of the Novel: French Fiction
since 1990.
Fiction Now: The French Novel in
the 21st Century.
Oulipo: A Primer of Potential
Literature.
GERALD MURNANE, *Barley Patch.*
Inland.

YVES NAVARRE, *Our Share of Time.*
Sweet Tooth.
DOROTHY NELSON, *In Night's City.*
Tar and Feathers.
ESHKOL NEVO, *Homesick.*
WILFRIDO D. NOLLEDO, *But for the Lovers.*
FLANN O'BRIEN, *At Swim-Two-Birds.*
At War.
The Best of Myles.
The Dalkey Archive.
Further Cuttings.
The Hard Life.
The Poor Mouth.
The Third Policeman.
CLAUDE OLLIER, *The Mise-en-Scène.*
Wert and the Life Without End.
GIOVANNI ORELLI, *Walaschek's Dream.*
PATRIK OUŘEDNÍK, *Europeana.*
The Opportune Moment, 1855.
BORIS PAHOR, *Necropolis.*
FERNANDO DEL PASO, *News from the Empire.*
Palinuro of Mexico.
ROBERT PINGET, *The Inquisitory.*
Mahu or The Material.
Trio.
A. G. PORTA, *The No World Concerto.*
MANUEL PUIG, *Betrayed by Rita Hayworth.*
The Buenos Aires Affair.
Heartbreak Tango.
RAYMOND QUENEAU, *The Last Days.*
Odile.
Pierrot Mon Ami.
Saint Glinglin.
ANN QUIN, *Berg.*
Passages.
Three.
Tripticks.
ISHMAEL REED, *The Free-Lance Pallbearers.*
The Last Days of Louisiana Red.
Ishmael Reed: The Plays.
Juice!
Reckless Eyeballing.
The Terrible Threes.
The Terrible Twos.
Yellow Back Radio Broke-Down.
JASIA REICHARDT, *15 Journeys from Warsaw*
to London.
NOËLLE REVAZ, *With the Animals.*
JOÃO UBALDO RIBEIRO, *House of the*
Fortunate Buddhas.
JEAN RICARDOU, *Place Names.*
RAINER MARIA RILKE, *The Notebooks of*
Malte Laurids Brigge.
JULIÁN RÍOS, *The House of Ulysses.*
Larva: A Midsummer Night's Babel.
Poundemonium.
Procession of Shadows.
AUGUSTO ROA BASTOS, *I the Supreme.*
DANIËL ROBBERECHTS, *Arriving in Avignon.*
JEAN ROLIN, *The Explosion of the*
Radiator Hose.
OLIVIER ROLIN, *Hotel Crystal.*
ALIX CLEO ROUBAUD, *Alix's Journal.*
JACQUES ROUBAUD, *The Form of a*
City Changes Faster, Alas, Than
the Human Heart.
The Great Fire of London.
Hortense in Exile.
Hortense Is Abducted.
The Loop.
Mathematics:
The Plurality of Worlds of Lewis.

The Princess Hoppy.
Some Thing Black.
LEON S. ROUDIEZ, *French Fiction Revisited.*
RAYMOND ROUSSEL, *Impressions of Africa.*
VEDRANA RUDAN, *Night.*
STIG SÆTERBAKKEN, *Siamese.*
LYDIE SALVAYRE, *The Company of Ghosts.*
Everyday Life.
The Lecture.
*Portrait of the Writer as a
Domesticated Animal.*
The Power of Flies.
LUIS RAFAEL SÁNCHEZ,
Macho Camacho's Beat.
SEVERO SARDUY, *Cobra & Maitreya.*
NATHALIE SARRAUTE,
Do You Hear Them?
Martereau.
The Planetarium.
ARNO SCHMIDT, *Collected Novellas.*
Collected Stories.
Nobodaddy's Children.
Two Novels.
ASAF SCHURR, *Motti.*
CHRISTINE SCHUTT, *Nightwork.*
GAIL SCOTT, *My Paris.*
DAMION SEARLS, *What We Were Doing
and Where We Were Going.*
JUNE AKERS SEESE,
Is This What Other Women Feel Too?
What Waiting Really Means.
BERNARD SHARE, *Inish.*
Transit.
AURELIE SHEEHAN, *Jack Kerouac Is Pregnant.*
VIKTOR SHKLOVSKY, *Bowstring.*
Knight's Move.
*A Sentimental Journey:
Memoirs 1917–1922.*
Energy of Delusion: A Book on Plot.
Literature and Cinematography.
Theory of Prose.
Third Factory.
Zoo, or Letters Not about Love.
CLAUDE SIMON, *The Invitation.*
PIERRE SINIAC, *The Collaborators.*
KJERSTI A. SKOMSVOLD, *The Faster I Walk,
the Smaller I Am.*
JOSEF ŠKVORECKÝ, *The Engineer of
Human Souls.*
GILBERT SORRENTINO,
Aberration of Starlight.
Blue Pastoral.
Crystal Vision.
*Imaginative Qualities of Actual
Things.*
Mulligan Stew.
Pack of Lies.
Red the Fiend.
The Sky Changes.
Something Said.
Splendide-Hôtel.
Steelwork.
Under the Shadow.
W. M. SPACKMAN, *The Complete Fiction.*
ANDRZEJ STASIUK, *Dukla.*
Fado.
GERTRUDE STEIN, *Lucy Church Amiably.*
The Making of Americans.
A Novel of Thank You.
LARS SVENDSEN, *A Philosophy of Evil.*
PIOTR SZEWC, *Annihilation.*
GONÇALO M. TAVARES, *Jerusalem.*

Joseph Walser's Machine.
*Learning to Pray in the Age of
Technique.*
LUCIAN DAN TEODOROVICI,
Our Circus Presents . . .
NIKANOR TERATOLOGEN, *Assisted Living.*
STEFAN THEMERSON, *Hobson's Island.*
The Mystery of the Sardine.
Tom Harris.
TAEKO TOMIOKA, *Building Waves.*
JOHN TOOMEY, *Sleepwalker.*
JEAN-PHILIPPE TOUSSAINT, *The Bathroom.*
Camera.
Monsieur.
Reticence.
Running Away.
Self-Portrait Abroad.
Television.
The Truth about Marie.
DUMITRU TSEPENEAG, *Hotel Europa.*
The Necessary Marriage.
Pigeon Post.
Vain Art of the Fugue.
ESTHER TUSQUETS, *Stranded.*
DUBRAVKA UGRESIC, *Lend Me Your Character.*
Thank You for Not Reading.
TOR ULVEN, *Replacement.*
MATI UNT, *Brecht at Night.*
Diary of a Blood Donor.
Things in the Night.
ÁLVARO URIBE AND OLIVIA SEARS, EDS.,
Best of Contemporary Mexican Fiction.
ELOY URROZ, *Friction.*
The Obstacles.
LUISA VALENZUELA, *Dark Desires and
the Others.*
He Who Searches.
MARJA-LIISA VARTIO, *The Parson's Widow.*
PAUL VERHAEGHEN, *Omega Minor.*
AGLAJA VETERANYI, *Why the Child Is
Cooking in the Polenta.*
BORIS VIAN, *Heartsnatcher.*
LLORENÇ VILLALONGA, *The Dolls' Room.*
TOOMAS VINT, *An Unending Landscape.*
ORNELA VORPSI, *The Country Where No
One Ever Dies.*
AUSTRYN WAINHOUSE, *Hedyphagetica.*
PAUL WEST, *Words for a Deaf Daughter
& Gala.*
CURTIS WHITE, *America's Magic Mountain.*
The Idea of Home.
Memories of My Father Watching TV.
*Monstrous Possibility: An Invitation
to Literary Politics.*
Requiem.
DIANE WILLIAMS, *Excitability:
Selected Stories.*
Romancer Erector.
DOUGLAS WOOLF, *Wall to Wall.*
Ya! & John-Juan.
JAY WRIGHT, *Polynomials and Pollen.*
*The Presentable Art of Reading
Absence.*
PHILIP WYLIE, *Generation of Vipers.*
MARGUERITE YOUNG, *Angel in the Forest.*
Miss MacIntosh, My Darling.
REYOUNG, *Unbabbling.*
VLADO ŽABOT, *The Succubus.*
ZORAN ŽIVKOVIĆ, *Hidden Camera.*
LOUIS ZUKOFSKY, *Collected Fiction.*
VITOMIL ZUPAN, *Minuet for Guitar.*
SCOTT ZWIREN, *God Head.*